T0345568

Mahasweta Devi (1926–2016) was one of India's foremost literary personalities, a prolific and bestselling author in Bengali of short fiction and novels; a deeply political social activist who worked with and for Adivasi people and marginalized communities such as the landless labourers of eastern India for years; the editor of a quarterly, *Bortika*, in which marginalized people themselves documented grassroots-level issues; and a sociopolitical commentator whose articles appeared regularly in the *Economic and Political Weekly*, *Frontier* and other journals.

Mahasweta Devi's empirical research into oral history as it lives in the cultures and memories of Adivasi communities was a first of its kind. Her powerful, haunting tales of exploitation and struggle have been seen as rich sites of feminist discourse by leading scholars. Her innovative use of language has expanded the conventional borders of Bengali literary expression. Standing at the intersection of vital contemporary questions of politics, gender and class, she remains a significant figure in the field of socially committed literature.

Recognizing this, Seagull Books has conceived a publishing programme which encompasses a representational look at the complete Mahasweta: her novels, her short fiction, her children's stories, her plays, her activist prose writings. The series is an attempt to introduce her impressive body of work to a readership beyond Bengal; it is also an overdue recognition of the importance of her contribution to the literary and cultural history of India.

THE INDIA LIST

MAHASWETA DEVI

The Murderer's Mother

Translated by Arunava Sinha

LONDON NEW YORK CALCUTTA

Seagull Books, 2023

Originally published in Bengali as
Murderer-er Maa (Kolkata: Dey's Publishing, 1992)
Currently available in *Mahasweta Devi Rachanasamagra*, VOL. 20
[Collected works of Mahasweta Devi] (Kolkata: Dey's Publishing, 2004)

© Tathagata Bhattacharya

First published in English translation by Seagull Books, 2023
English translation © Arunava Sinha, 2023

ISBN 978 1 80309 232 4

British Library Cataloguing-in-Publication Data
A catalogue record for this book is available from the British Library

Typeset by Seagull Books, Calcutta, India
Printed and bound by Hyam Enterprises, Calcutta, India

For
Smt. Mukul Mukhopadhyay
and Dr Arunprasad Mukhopadhyay

At night, Rani could barely keep her eyes open after eleven. She felt so sleepy all the time. But in the byarakbaari, no one would let Rani, or any of the other Ranis, go to bed so early. They had to sit and wait, wait and wait, wearing their glittering maxi-gowns or kurta–pyjamas or Bombay film-star-style dresses. And then they had to take them off. Take them off night after night, day after day. Why the Ranis of the world had to strip naked like this since time immemorial, Rani didn't know. Did anyone know?

This town in the North 24 Parganas district was very close to Calcutta. And this barrack-like building—everyone called it the byarakbaari—was in a part of the town that was easy to enter but impossible to exit. While the rest of the town fell asleep, this building buzzed with activity. Videos ran all night long in five different rooms. There was a hooch den, there was a drug den. And there were the Ranis.

It was an empire which yielded a great deal of revenue. Its emperor was Tiger. Here, when the emperor dies, his son doesn't succeed him. Someone else grows more powerful, wrests away control after a fierce struggle. One-armed Dinu had built the empire during the Congress rule. One still heard talk of his many exploits. Apparently, on Netaji's birthday, he made the slum children do mock military drills. He owned a motorcycle and an Ambassador car, but chose to get about in a cycle rickshaw. He owned the byarakbaari, the girls too. Still, he had let Chhobi go.

Rani and the rest of the girls often gossiped with the madam, they called her Mashi. Rani loved listening to the story about Chhobi.

Chhobi was new here, she hadn't mastered the trade yet. Mashi said: She still smelt of the fields and farms, she cried a lot.

–How did she get away?

–That's a strange story.

–What happened?

*

In those days, every night at ten, Dinu would come to Mashi's room to drink. He never spent a night there. No matter how late it was, if he was in the town, he always went home. His house was in the town, on the other side of the railway line. He had the house his father had built, had a beautiful wife, had a son. He kept a bodyguard, he had to. The bodyguard's name was Irani. That night too, like all the other nights, Dinu was about to leave at eleven, after his drinks. Chhobi had just seen off a client, she was still standing at the door. On his way out, Dinu's shoe-clad foot knocked against her. 'Who's that, Ma?' he blurted out, 'I didn't see you, I didn't mean to.'

Mashi had burst out laughing. 'Who are you calling Ma, babu? That's Chhobi, that girl from Champbere. The one that caused so much trouble in the summer. The one that keeps trying to run away.'

Chhobi was trembling. The very name 'Dinu-babu' sent shivers down her spine. Apparently, one roar from him could frighten a pregnant woman into a premature delivery. He summoned people, lined them up before him, then shot them point blank. Chhobi was trembling, tears streaming down her face.

Dinu shook his head two or three times to clear his mind. Today has been a lucky day. In a stubborn fit, he'd once bought a luxury-taxi business. Just that day, he'd sold it at a fat profit. He was in a good mood. 'Did I say Ma?' he said. 'How did that word come to my lips? Must be Ma's wish. How hard I prayed to her before I offered her my puja. Dinu has no one, Ma, Dinu is so wretched. They say I've blackened the family's face. Ma! You can see how hard I'm struggling to climb my way up. Hear my prayers, Ma. Hear my prayers. I made my offering, she accepted my flowers. This can't have happened without her grace. My own Ma refuses to look at the bad young son's face, has gone off to live with the good elder son, where she's getting kicked around by his wife. I never go to see her. Keep all my heart's desires buried in my heart. But in that same heart I keep calling: Ma, Ma, Ma! And now that great big word has suddenly slipped out. What did you say? She'd run away?'

–Yes babu, not once but twice.

—Never mind. Now that I've said it . . . What do you know what Ma means, you whorehouse madam? Left your husband and became a whore. When your body broke, you became a madam. Whom can one call Ma? One's mother or one's daughter. Since I've called her Ma, I'll let her go.

Chhobi began to sob.

—Let her go? Where will she go? It's taken us this long to get her fangs out, she's finally growing tame . . .

—Shut up.

—Where will she go anyway? You think her parents will take her back?

—That's her problem. Listen, girl. I'll let you go. Put you on the train tomorrow. Don't even think of going to the police.

Dinu really did let Chhobi go. At the same time, an order was issued: No one was to stand at the door when Dinu-babu came or went. Babu's feet could slip again, he could call someone else Ma again. In that case, he would have to let her go again, because once he'd called a woman Ma, it was a grave sin to make money from her body. The word Ma was full of majesty, nobility. It was best for such accidents to occur only once. Otherwise, the trade would go belly up.

'Besides,' Mashi says, 'this is a business, after all. The business would have suffered.'

—He really let her go?

—I went to Sealdah and bought her ticket myself, put her on the train.

–And then?

–Who knows? Bilash from the paan shop said he'd seen her selling vegetables on the footpath outside Kolay Market. Who knows whom he saw? Everyone says they want to go. Go where? Will their parents take them back? Will anyone marry them? Even if they do go, they end up in the same business again. Pimps on the prowl everywhere. They pick them up and push them back into the line.

–And then?

–What do you think? The lucky ones become madams like me. The rest go to hell. Go to bed now. I need to sleep too. What are you worried about? As long as your body is young, you don't have to worry.

*

Dinu's authority lasted as long as the Congress was in power. He lost his left arm making bombs. The party leaders had visited him in hospital, addressed him as Dinu-babu. Top police officers would slap cases on him, but couldn't make any of them stick.

Then the Congress was out, and so was Dinu. Dinu was removed by Tapan. Dinu or Tapan or someone else, whoever was the recruit of the time. Recruited by the need of the hour, and by history, the way soldiers are recruited for war. War creates history, just as history creates war. In West Bengal, from the days of Gopal Pantha down to Ramen Mandal, and ever since, it has been the political history of the moment that has recruited them, armed them. These days, of course, the recruits have become even more essential. Politics no longer controls the antisocial elements. Instead, politics and the criminal industry support each other. The criminals had already seized several areas across the map of India. They fought elections, became leaders of the masses. What the masses think about all this, that is never taken into account. Never written about. Once the criminals were controlled by politics, Time, the writer of history, had armed them with switch-knives, revolvers, pistols and bombs. Now it has given them advanced firearms, more powerful bombs. This doesn't mean that the old knives or the old men have been flung aside. As a silent killer, the knife is still relevant and far from obsolete.

Tapan was the recruit of his time. A large section of youths was caught up in the frenzy of the Naxal movement then, and even before the Congress came to power in 1972, following a bloodbath of young Naxalites in the metropolis and elsewhere, several assassins had been created from among the half-educated, little-educated and uneducated apolitical young men in cities and towns, adrift on a sea of unemployment and despair. A number of 'antisocials' had now even become friends of the police, they were no longer the enemy.

For a price.

The police gave them money, and they gave their lives, their dignity, their right to live as humans. They weren't human any more.

Between 1972 and 1975, when many Naxalites were in jail and many others still free, the Congress government and the police jointly recruited many semi-educated trigger-happy young men. They were known as Congsals. Claiming to support the Naxal movement, they infiltrated the Naxalites on behalf of the Congress government. They were instructed to arbitrarily murder innocent people, murders that could not be explained and hence, could be blamed on the Naxalites. If such killings could continue, the common man's respect for the Naxal movement would slowly vanish, and it would be possible to publicize the idea that the Naxalites were murderers.

There was one more instruction: You will also be arrested as guilty Naxalites, and lodged in the same jail. There, you must befriend them, worm out as many of their secrets as possible. Sniff out plans for jailbreaks, find out who's gone underground and where.

Tapan was a Congsal. No matter how hard the Naxals were beaten up in jail, no stick ever landed on a Congsal's back. It was also true that the Naxals made no mistake in identifying the Congsals. They paid them no attention. As a result, this section of inmates became somewhat isolated. Released in 1977, the Congsals were rewarded for their faithful service with different kinds of jobs. Fit into different positions as per their qualifications.

Born with a malformed arm, Chhanu would at one time show it off as 'the result of police brutality during political activity'. When he later saw that no one believed his story, he shut up. When he was released from jail, his health much recovered, he took to selling chickens for a living.

Tapan belonged to a different category. He was handsome, had a winning smile and was highly regarded as a skilled knifer. He'd been to jail on the instruction of his leaders, the same leaders who introduced him to Malay in the town. Malay was part of Dinu's gang. But he was not happy with just that one hooch den. He thought of himself as 'oppressed and deprived', claimed to be a victim of upper-caste contempt. 'Dinu Ganguly is a brahman, he picks brahmans and kayasthas and gives them the better shares. I'm actually a Ruidas—Scheduled Caste. Why will he give me anything? But when it's risk your life and chuck a bomb, then it's got to be Malay. Didn't you see the fight with Punjab Singh the other day?'

Tapan had realized it wouldn't be hard to use Malay and then discard him.

Malay had said, 'In any case, Dinu-babu's been in business a long time. Ten years. Enough. Pension him off. It's our turn now.'

–Who'll do it?

–I can.

–No, you can't. Irani is a fighter.

–Because he uses a gun?

–No, he's dangerous.

–Then what? You think you can do it yourself? You've come here, sat in the tea shop, chatted with me. But all this belongs to Dinu-babu, don't forget. Ever done politics? Champak did politics. He was a Naxal.

–Don't talk crap, Malay. Champak studied with me.

–Hehe, he was a Naxal, you're a Congsal.

Tapan's eyes flashed. His hand stole to his pocket. Slicing Malay's belly wide open would be an easy solution. But while it may be easy, it was not necessarily a solution. Not for someone who didn't yet have a gang behind him. This would mean making himself vulnerable to many others, equally armed. And Tapan wasn't such a fool. He was merely one among many. A recruit of the times.

Bhabani-babu took him to meet Kanak Majumdar. IPS Kanak Majumdar, a dynamic young man. Fluent in English. Determined to purge the Naxals. He had made many a young man disappear forever. It was he who outlined the plan to Tapan.

Except, the plan wasn't put to use. Tapan was lodged in the same jail as Champak. But Champak denied all knowledge of him. Tapan was hurt to the core. 'You're not the Tapan I knew,' Champak said, 'fuck off.'

Champak and his group stuck together, sang together. Disobeyed the warden, protested against the inmates' food, their medical treatment. They were respected by the other convicts, who would ask them: What did you get by ruining your life?

No one had ever spoken to Tapan with such affection. After his release, Champak organized the press workers of the town into a union. He was a local favourite. But Bhabani-babu was not happy about the success of a Naxalite trade union. Soon after, Champak was murdered by an unidentified assailant.

Today, Tapan realized that had been Dinu's doing too. Malay hinted as much.

Dinu could not but be suspicious about how Tapan gained entry into the town.

Bhabani-babu had told Tapan, 'Dinu is where he is today because of me.'

–I know.

–You're also in this line because of me. Border town, business is booming, revenues will go past ten lakhs a month soon.

–What are you asking me to do?

–No use asking Irani. He listens to no one but Dinu.

–That's a plus quality, Bhabani-da, maybe one day you can rely on him.

–You're making a mistake. Irani will obey no one but Dinu.

–Will Malay do it?

–Malay, China, Badal . . .

–But can we depend on them? If they can betray Dinu, can't they betray me too?

Apparently Bhabani-babu had one glass eye, but it was impossible to tell which one. Both were expressionless, cold as stone. Bhabani-babu was not the king, he was the kingmaker. He could crown them, he could topple them too. He owned jute mills, workshops in the railyard, enormous slums.

Bhabani-babu was also from this town. A search might even reveal a family connection with Dinu-babu. His ancestors had built a number of Sanskrit grammar schools on the banks of the Ganga. The last case of sati was rumoured to have been in his family. The river had long since changed its course, far from the location of the sati pyre. A brick kiln stood there now.

Bhabani-babu's father Rajani-babu had been a Gandhian, a veteran Congress supporter. His sons, quite naturally, remained in the Congress camp. The first three sons were well-established lawyers in Calcutta, they no longer came to this town. Because of Bhabani-babu.

Bhabani-babu had not bothered to get an education. In his youth, he had opened a hooch den in the coolie slums, and then, robbing a jute mill, had absconded with the money. Rajani-babu had disowned him. But as soon as he died, Bhabani came back and set up a Congress union in the same jute mill. Set up the hooch and gambling dens, the band of goons called the Youth Squad. He was a pioneer in whatever he did. He became so powerful that it was impossible to win a seat in the State Assembly without his support.

But even this Bhabani got married. Because in India, whether they be murderers or lechers, all men find a wife. Bhabani-babu had no time for his wife. She was a feisty woman, and many were the people who overheard their quarrels. That was when Bhabani-babu became increasingly intimate with the woman who was now the madam at the byarakbaari. Bhabani-babu's wife strongly objected to this. Then, suddenly, she died in a fire. People suspected the death hadn't been entirely accidental. That very evening she'd been to the Kali Puja celebrations in the neighbour-hood. Then at dawn it was heard that the night before, around eleven, she'd been heating food on a kerosene stove and then she burnt to death.

The cremation was carried out that morning itself, quite early. The police did not turn up, nor was there a post-mortem. But talk spread like wildfire. Everyone said that burning wives was not so common these days, Bhabani-babu was a pioneer in that too.

There was no telling whether Bhabani-babu heard any of this.

He didn't marry again. Apparently, he went on a pilgrimage for a few months. Then came back in a new avatar: 'I'm going into politics.' He set up office at home, needed a new Youth Squad, so he built up a new team of mastaans. Became an advisor to the trade unions. Held regular tripartite discussions with the owners of mills and factories and the government's labour department. Gradually, he became the most powerful man in town, its controller. The boss.

Bhabani-babu explained to Tapan that Dinu didn't understand politics, he only understood mastaan and muscles. But there was a new government in the state now, and it understood politics. 'People have voted them in,' said Bhabani-babu. 'We have to be careful now. We've ruled over them for a long time, run riot, done a lot of things. That's not possible any more.'

– They're the ones who've cast us aside, Bhabani-da.

– Naturally. They're the ones here to stay.

– So were you and your party.

– Yes, but we made mistakes.

– Will you correct them now?

– Gradually. We've done anti-people things too. I regret it now. We let an antisocial like Dinu . . .

Tapan understood. Create an antisocial, use him, discard him. Create another one. To survive this game, you had to be strong enough to combat politicians like Bhabani-babu.

Now we are the ones who need them, Tapan thought.

We have to create such a situation that their need is greater. Then, we'll have the upper hand.

That day isn't here yet, not yet.

'Won't you give Dinu-babu a chance?' said Tapan. He thought: Dinu-babu had served Bhabani-babu well.

– What are you saying? Are you mad?

– You could pay him, get him to leave. Go somewhere else.

–Dinu won't go.

–Still . . .

With a rap on his hand, Bhabani-babu said, 'There's a new government now, we have to adopt new ways. Have to rip off the Congress label. Does Dinu have brains enough for that? He's a Congress thug. You really think he should be given a chance? Such things happen only in novels and plays. Ever since you read some books, your brains have . . .'

–I've hardly read any books.

–You have to be careful now.

Or Bhabani-babu would send for some other Tapan. Discard this one. It was clear Bhabani-babu was preparing to swiftly change course.

–Are you a paragon of virtue yourself? It's not like you haven't murdered anyone.

–I have.

Can Tapan ever forget his first step down the road of darkness? In 1970, he'd been just twenty. But since he'd passed his Class Ten exams, there'd been nothing but abuse at home. His father was a clerk at the bus office, came home drunk every night. His mother was a hospital ayah. She didn't indulge Tapan's three younger siblings with any attempt at an education. The two brothers became apprentice cleaners at the bus garage. And their sister—Tapan's mother got her a job, looking after a doctor's baby.

Tapan used to get into fights, sell movie tickets on the black market. He had understood all too well that he would never land a job.

Champak came from a decent family, he went to Calcutta to study. He used to tell Tapan, 'Why are you letting your life go to hell like this?

–What else can I do?

–Some other kind of work?

–I'm not like you. Have you seen my family? It's because of my daily diet of misery that I'm in this business now.

Getting off his cycle, Champak would wag his finger at Tapan and explain that it was all the result of this fake independence. People were becoming poorer, working so hard and still going hungry. Society was rotting, falling apart. And young men like Tapan, yet to be ruined, were its victims.

–That's all very well. If only like you I had a father with a government job and a schoolteacher mother, I might have thought the same. Forget about it.

–Do you want to go to college?

–What's the point? Do you know how many people from the town are already registered at the Naihati Employment Exchange?

–That doesn't mean you sell movie tickets on the black market.

–Why not? My clothes and expenses, I'm earning enough for myself.

–Isn't it possible to make an honest living?

–No, it's not. Dr Avinash buys only the cheapest vegetables in the market. No one takes his homoeopathy pills. Dr Robi, on the other hand, doles out plain white tablets, but plays the 'homeopath by divine direction' card. And eats mutton every day. Yet, they're brothers, the two of them. Come with me to town, I'll show you.

–Not even a job in a primary school?

–Father's famous in town as Drunkard Gopal, mother's a maid in a hospital. Who's going to give their son a schoolteacher's job? How much do those jobs pay anyway?

–I don't know what to say.

–Say nothing.

–Sourav's going to college, isn't he?

'What use will that be?' snapped Tapan, his words dripping with contempt, 'Sourav makes bidis, does tuitions, to be able to afford college. But what good will that do? Do you know how many BAs and MAs are unemployed? When a hit movie is released, I can make up to twenty bucks a day. Can Sourav make anything like that?'

–Talking to you is . . .

–Pointless. Best not to, Champak. People will hate you if they see you talking to me.

–Whatever you do, don't become a goonda.

–Goondas have a good life Champak, look at Dinu Ganguly. Look at his car, see how his pocket bulges with notes.

–No! You mustn't choose that road.

Who chooses the road? The road chooses you. Tapan seemed to have lost all his patience by the time he was twenty. He'd be furious all the time. He'd feel suffocated by this town. He'd be filled with loathing at the thought of going back home. Every day his father would say, 'Pretends he doesn't know me when he sees me on the street. Hates me. If he hates us so much, why does he stay? Let him get out, fend for himself.'

His mother would say, 'If he truly hated us, he'd have been gone by now.'

*

It wasn't just Champak who kept an eye on him, Bhabani-babu did too. That was the time when the legendary battle took place, between Tapan and his boys and the gang that organized the famous Lyalka Jute Mill Durga Puja. Several of them had driven up in a jeep to avenge the humiliation of a woman on their puja-pandal precincts. Armed with hockey sticks, all of them molly-coddled sons of officers. Tapan thrashed them single-handed, armed with only a bamboo pole. The incident had long-lasting effects, because the goondas who turned up with bombs on the night of Kali Puja to avenge that thrashing were no longer soft boys but hired hands, professionals. They had been brought in because they were thought to be 'more than enough' to beat up Tapan and his group, the young Milanmela men.

Tapan and his group, though, were by no means unprepared. In the battle that ensued under his leadership, Jagan lost an arm, the jeep was set on fire, its driver was killed, and the police came.

With the driver dying, the police labelled Tapan a murderer. But to his utter surprise, Bhabani-babu went to the lockup and had him released. Told the officer, 'It was a battle between Bengalis and non-Bengalis, and the Bengali boys vanquished evil. How could you arrest him? Charged with murder! Who saw him commit a murder?'

To Tapan, he said, 'Well done, my boy.'

Then, taking Tapan home, he plied him with enormous sweets. 'The idol has been damaged,' he said, 'I'll do the atonement puja myself this time, for Milanmela.'

Tucking two thousand rupees into Tapan's pocket for the ceremonies, and another five hundred with a 'keep it, keep it for yourself', Bhabani-babu more or less bought Tapan on the spot. The five-hundred rupee note injected such exhilaration in Tapan's blood, such an ebullience in his heart.

Still, Tapan said, 'No need for money.'

–Why not, what's the matter?

–Give me a job instead.

–Of course I will. Consider it done. Start tomorrow.

–What job, Dada?

–Enemies everywhere, everywhere, understand? You'll be with me, be my right hand. Five hundred a month, seven hundred, name your figure. But you'll have to forget about your home. You'll stay here, eat here, sleep here. All right?

The fire of the five hundred rupees sparked a flame inside Tapan. The money was assured. Tapan began to dream. Life was turning into a movie. Five hundred today, five thousand tomorrow, everything was possible. He began to think of Bhabani-babu as a great man indeed.

Tapan went home with ten rupees' worth of sweets and fifteen of fish. He would have to astonish his family.

*

His mother was speechless. 'Let Reba quit her job,' he told her. 'Suku and Buku too.'

–Are you mad?

–Take this money, you'll get it every month. Let Reba stay at home, she's grown up now.

–Have you got a job?

–Work. I'll work, I'll get paid, I'll give you money. You thought I'd gone to hell.

–You know how it is. I know I've said horrible things, I was so frustrated.

–No need to worry any more. How's the fish, Ma—is it good?

–Of course it is! Just look at it!

–I'll work, eat fish every day.

Tapan's happy dreams were very simple that day. Everyone would eat fish every day, Suku and Buku would get some professional training, Reba would go to school. Just that much was good enough.

Tapan's father came out of his room.

–Give something to your father too?

'So you can drink?' Tapan's mother said.

–Shut up, bitch.

Tapan was still in the grip of a different elation. Flying into a rage, he said, 'I cracked three skulls the other night at the puja pandal, I can crack four too. Behave yourself. I'm warning you.'

–You'll beat up your father?

–If he's that kind of father, yes.

Tapan's father raged at him at the top of his voice, but eventually fell silent when he learnt that his son was now moving about in Bhabani-babu's car.

Tapan followed Bhabani-babu's instructions, and in only three months, in exchange for fat sums of money, he succeeded in evicting the old hawkers from the station market and installing new ones. He also beat up the secretary of the Hawkers' Union and packed him off to the hospital.

All this could be done in full view of the public. But when Bharat Bansphor started a movement against a hooch den being set up in the quarters for Dalit railway and hospital workers, Bhabani-babu felt Bansphor and his lot were going too far. 'The union's ours. We decide whom the railways hire. They're creating trouble about this. Your people are getting jobs on our quotas, they do none of the cleaning—we do. They only collect their salaries.'

Tapan smiled. 'We used to support them once.'

–But try and understand! Our boys won't get the jobs. They drink too. Then why is Bharat opposed to the den? We're making some people self-reliant by giving them a liquor business of their own, what's wrong with that?

–They're molesting these people's women too.

–Lies, Tapan, all lies. Bharat Bansphor thinks he's a great leader. They've even put together a team to beat people up.

–What are you asking me to do?

–Take him out.

–Bharat? I used to play football with them.

–So?

–Bharat . . . Out of the blue . . .

–Bharat is a nuisance.

–He's hot-headed. Shouts too much, but gutsy, uses his fists only when he must. I've known him a long time.

–Are you aware that Bharat is a rioter?

But he doesn't kill, Tapan thought to himself. Still, it was he who killed Bharat. The whole thing happened somehow. God knew Tapan didn't go to warn Bharat's sister that afternoon with the intention of murdering him.

Bharat's sister Chameli was about twenty-two, the mother of two children, a sweeper at the hospital. Bharat lived with his sister, drove a rickshaw, had connections at the employment exchange, might get a job any day now. He had stopped studying after Class Eight because he wanted to get some vocational training instead. But with no work to be had, with none of the positions reserved for the Scheduled Castes actually available, Bharat's head had begun to fill with rage. He began to see injustice everywhere. 'The sixes and fives have all been flung aside,' he told Chameli, 'it's a three-card game now. Don't tell me this isn't right or that isn't right. Who's doing what's right by me? Why must I do what's right by anyone else?'

–You get married now.

–Open toilets, drink and drugs everywhere, a shanty for a home, no good way to live anywhere. And a wife and child in the middle of all this?

Bharat was a Dalit, he wanted to live as one too. But as a civilized human, not rotting in a slum till his death. He had spent much of his time organizing protests outside the employment exchange, shouting 'Where are the reserved quotas?' 'Naihati Exchange, answer us!' He had wanted to unite the Dalits.

He never acknowledged Tapan when he ran into him, ignored him entirely. So Tapan had no choice but to visit Chameli. 'Tell Bharat that the boss is keeping an eye on him, Chameli,' he said, 'he'd better not wander about alone at night. He won't talk to me, so I'm telling you.'

–His heart is filled with sorrow after sorrow. That's why he's so angry all the time. Didn't get a single job anywhere.

–Why doesn't he take it up with the railway union?

–That's Bhabani-babu's union.

–That's true. I'll see if I can get him a job at a shoe shop in Jagaddal.

–All right.

–But tell him what I said. My intentions are good. If he could just get away . . .

Chameli must have passed on the message accurately. Their father, Dhanu Bansphor, used to be part of the Ambedkar Mission. He was a little different from the rest, he'd sent his children to school, he didn't drink or do drugs, he had even started a movement against drinking at weddings. He made beautiful kites. It was Dhanu's kites that Tapan and his friends would fly during Vishwakarma Puja.

Tapan could not gauge just how dangerous Bharat had become for Bhabani-babu. It was true that although the Dalit shanties had been built on railway land, neither the municipality nor the railway corporation had made any effort to develop them. Open toilets, the slums right next to them, nothing but pigsties. And it was also true that, at different places inside those slums, the goondas had set up their hooch shops.

Hooch selling and drinking. Brawling. Molesting women. Bharat and his companions had complained repeatedly to the police station, to the elected representatives, but to no avail.

Was Champak helping Bharat on the sly? Tapan had warned Chameli that Bharat should watch his step.

Bhabani-babu would suspect Tapan if he came to know. Right now, Bhabani-babu was more interested in getting Dinu-babu out of the picture and handing over the town to Tapan so that he could control everything from behind the scenes.

So Bhabani-babu wouldn't get rid of Tapan just yet—he would give him a chance. When Tapan finally became super-annuated like Dinu-babu, then he would have to step aside. Step aside, meaning: be erased. Who could step aside and still stay alive? Tapan had no choice but to do this task. Bharat! I'm giving you a chance. Then, if need be . . . unless you mind your ways. When my blood dances, so does my switch-knife. It's not my hand that grips the knife—it's the knife that leaps into my hand. Controls me.

Bhabani-babu is my controller. Dinu-babu's, too. One day, with me as a front, Bhabani-babu will be the controller of this town.

This is how this town's history will be, for now. At one time, there were huge labour unions here. Many protests, many processions. Life had a certain flow back then. The labour leaders addressed everyone as 'comrade'. Anyone who was close to the police back then didn't dare show their faces in public.

Now the police station is our second home. It is no longer condemnable to have a direct line to the police. In fact, it is a matter of pride. When something goes wrong, people run around, desperately seeking someone with a line to the police. The thing is, no matter which line you run to, they all lead to Bhabani-babu.

*

Tapan was on his way back home that evening after a cup of tea at the station when Shobuj came up to him. He sold movie tickets on the black market, while his twin Shyamal was active in Champak's press-workers' union. Bhabani-babu was the boss, Dinu-babu was the dada, but it was still Champak's town. They were the shock of the countercurrent. They had their own cultural platform, their folk-music group—they even observed Champak's death anniversary. Shyamal and his friends staged plays in the Dalit slums, sang songs for them. As for the incident concerning Bharat Bansphor, that happened much later.

'Just a minute, Tapan-da,' said Shobuj.

Tapan got off his cycle. Does Shobuj know that Tapan won't be using a cycle much longer, that he'll be riding a motorcycle soon? Eat fish and meat every day? Take the prettiest girls in town to the movies? Perhaps he did.

–What is it, Shobuj?

Shobuj cast a quick look around, then said, 'Bharat-da's asking to see you. In the church field.'

–When?

–After the show. He's watching *Ustad*.

–Right now?

–Yes, he prefers the evening show. Then locks up the night school.

–What's Shyamal up to?

–He's around.

Tapan mulled things over on his way home. He was important at home now, he'd given his mother some money, he'd give more. She gave him hot rotis and a cup of tea, and said, 'Bhabani-babu's sent for you.'

*

26

'Why did you go to Chameli's?' Bhabani-babu said.

–To check on Bharat.

–I have news that he's turned into a real son-of-a-bitch. Used to hang around with Champak's men too.

–Bharat? I don't believe it.

–You don't believe me?

–Who's giving you all this news?

–I have to keep up, Tapan. I have to keep up with you too.

–Me? What about me?

–Are you going to meet him?

–Who told you?

–The same person who told you. I have people everywhere in the town, Tapan. You'll find out in time. Go meet Bharat. Here's your chance. Make use of it.

Tapan was startled.

–Get it done, I'll take care of things afterwards.

–But a cold-blooded . . .

–Your hands will do the job, not your head.

–What if I can explain things to him? Why kill him, he might prove useful to us?

If only Bharat would understand, Tapan was thinking, it might help. Those childhood memories of flying kites, should he murder his own childhood now? How?

–That would be good, very good. Are you afraid?

–No, I'm not afraid.

*

Bharat must have grown impatient to be murdered. The church field was put to various uses these days. There were large trees on it, roadrollers too. Bharat was leaning against a tree.

–Bharat.

–You fucking Congsal! Why'd you go to my sister?

–To warn you.

–Why, will you kill me?

–I don't want to. You'd better fuck off.

Bharat grunted like a wild boar.

–Why should I fuck off? I'm from the town, never taken money to cause trouble. You antisocials, you can fuck off. The town will be clean again.

–I'm giving you some money, Bharat. Just go away for a few days.

–I don't listen to bastards.

–We used to play together . . .

–You people want the Dalits to take to drink, you want to molest their women, you're the ones who should fuck off.

–You're not even willing to listen?

–No. Even if I was, why should I listen to you lot? You think you can simply carry on with the hooch shops?

–What did you call me here for?

–To teach you a lesson.

–What sort of lesson?

–The kind your father taught Rabi Das of the sweepers' union. You have many fathers now. Gopal-babu, Bhabani-babu, Dinu-babu, Officer-babu . . . I don't have any fucking fathers, I'm an orphan.

–Bharat!

–Go, go back to your father.

–No, you must listen to me before you leave.

Tapan grabbed Bharat's collar. Bharat had been seething for a long time, a rage had been brewing inside him for days.

–You dare touch me, you bastard!

Tapan gave him a shove. But Bharat had a heavy torch in his pocket. He struck Tapan's forehead with it. 'One of us has to die today. You'll die, Tapan. Or you'll kill too many people in this town.'

Blood spurted out. 'Bharat! Bharat!' Tapan tended to go into a frenzy at the sight of blood, his own blood. Yet, he didn't reach for the switch-knife strapped to his ankle. For some time, they fought like beasts. In silence. Bharat kept pushing him, pushing him back.

–I don't know why Bhabani-babu has sent you!

Bharat had grabbed him by the throat now. How long could Tapan tighten his neck muscles and keep Bharat at bay? He kneed Bharat in the belly with all his might and threw him to the ground. Then he reached for his knife.

There was scant light filtering through the trees. Tapan lunged. Now it was impossible for both of them to return. Two men had come, only one man would leave.

In skilled hands, the knife was a silent assassin. Bharat slumped to the ground. Wiping the blade on the dry grass, Tapan folded it back and strapped it to his ankle again. Exhaling, he rose to his feet. It wasn't really a public place, though he had no idea who would be here in the morning. Tapan mounted his cycle.

*

Bhabani-babu's house.

Bhabani-babu's not home. Tiger is. He used to be Taraknath. Now he was Tiger.

–Where's Bhabani-da?

–In Calcutta. Come.

–Where?

–To Calcutta. I've got a car waiting.

Tapan got into the car, and vomited. Bharat, so he had killed Bharat? Did Bharat hate him so much? Bharat was gone, gone. Tapan had murdered his own childhood. Who would trust him any more?

And so to Calcutta. To spend a month or so out of sight, in Tiger's sister's house in Garia. Her husband was part-owner of a car workshop. She lived with her mother-in-law and daughter. Apparently, some of Bhabani-babu's cars were also given out on rent here.

'It's safe here,' Tiger said, 'stay here, hang out in the garage. Dada will send for you when it's time.'

Tapan spent a month relaxing. Grew a beard, grew his hair out. 'You're a Hindi-movie hero now,' Tiger's brother-in-law said.

True. His life seemed just as unreal. But no one really died when you used a knife in the movies. The hero could forget all about it after the scene had been shot. How was Tapan to forget Bharat?

Every night for a month, Bharat appeared in his dreams, holding kites. They ran about in the fields, flying their kites.

–I didn't want to kill you, Bharat.

–Then why did you?

–You wouldn't listen.

–Why did you bring a knife?

–I didn't want to take it out.

31

–You didn't?

–No . . . no . . .

Tapan would wake up screaming. 'Turn over on your side, Dada, drink some water,' Tiger's brother-in-law would say.

*

Tiger would bring all the news.

It was the slum-dwellers who discovered Bharat's body in the morning. Then Dhanu-babu junior and Shib-babu from the Dalit school rushed to the police station. Chameli had said, 'Tapan had been asking about him.' But his family said, 'Tapan left town last evening.'

*

–Where has Bhabani-babu gone?

–Siliguri. He's started his own business. When he returns, it'll be from Siliguri.

–How's the situation in the town?

–Shyamal's group is extremely active. Took out a procession. Some people from Calcutta joined too. Uproar outside the police station: The antisocials must be weeded out, et cetera. Even gave a memo to the OC—the Officer-in-Charge.

–Memorandum.

–Same thing.

–Any results?

–What results? The party's in the picture. We've given a written statement, told them Bharat had a hooch business. Some profit-and-loss argument must have led to the murder.

–What's Bhabani-da saying?

–He's asked you to keep quiet.

–You people sell hooch too.

–Bomba, Thaku, Rongeen and I. Cent-per cent profit.

–Anything else?

–He's sent an envelope.

Tiger handed it over. Five thousand rupees. Bharat's life was not worth much. The risk Tapan had taken was not worth much either. How much did Bhabani-babu make from hooch?

–How much do you give your Bhabani-da?

–He gets his share. We pay him first. Your time will come too. You'll have to pay him first as well. Dinu-babu doesn't understand this, he wants three-fourths for himself.

–Do you sister and brother-in-law know?

–Yes, they know everything.

–Aren't your parents alive?

–They are, they live near the Malda border.

–Do *they* know everything?

–Why shouldn't they? They didn't give their children an education, yet they're earning. You think they can't tell where the money's coming from? But do you know which line is truly no-investment-all-profit?

–Which?

–The woman line. Raw material everywhere. Select, pick up, supply.

Tiger was fidgeting.

–Something you want to say?

–Say what? You know about Shyamal?

–Know what?

–Your sister . . .

–Who said?

–Everyone knows.

–To hell with it. I wasn't keeping an eye on her, didn't take the responsibility either. If she marries him . . .

–Bhabani-babu doesn't want that.

–I'll see.

Reba was Tapan's sister, after all. Tapan's mother had been an ayah in a hospital. Reba used to work in a lady-doctor's quarters in return for food and clothing. Good food and good clothes had transformed her. Shyamal's family lived nearby, he and Shobuj were the sons of a wound dresser. Tapan didn't know how Shyamal drifted towards politics while Shobuj began selling movie tickets on the black market. Reba and Shyamal? A romance? Tapan hadn't been aware. He hardly spoke either to Reba or to their younger brothers Suku and Buku. Shyamal's parents had died a few years ago.

Tapan's brothers had chosen lines of work on their own.

Suku was a skilled electrician and repaired radios.

Buku sold Joy Bangla clothes in Bongaon.

Both of them had left home, and gone far away. Just as well. Even if Tapan saw better days, he didn't want his brothers to live with him.

He didn't make any attempt to get to know the people with whom he spent that month. Tiger's sister would bring him his food. She still called her brother Tarak, didn't she know his name was Tiger now?

Every evening, she would help her son with his studies. Apparently, the parents have to work hard to get their children into good schools. This was an unknown world for Tapan. Tiger's sister and brother-in-law never fought with each other. Tapan had never known a conjugal relationship like this. Tiger's sister was on good terms with her mother-in-law too, she made sure to keep everyone happy.

'Ran away from home not once but twice,' Tiger said. 'Finally, she met this one and stuck to him. You can see for yourself what a nice man Biren is. So I built him the garage, and then got them married. All thanks to Bhabani-da.'

–Do they own this house?

–They don't and they do. The owner will never be able to get them out, not in this lifetime. She's asthmatic, son lives in America. On top of that, the old woman's such a fool, she's filed a case against them. It's gone to court, a civil suit. But this house will come to them in the end.

Tapan hadn't paid much attention to Tiger before this. His gaze was steady, ice-cold. His movements silent. About twenty-five or twenty-six. He had come from the Nepal border, done several murders already. Tapan knew he had killed someone in Dhanbad and then sought shelter with Bhabani-babu. You had to be careful of a man like him, but as a human being he wasn't someone you had to be wary of.

And yet the same Tiger was so attentive to his sister and her son. How strange!

–Has your father built a house?

–Excellent exchange property, Dada. In the village, though almost a semi-town now. Two bighas of land, mango orchard, one-storeyed building. Baba has built it all.

–That's good, isn't it?

–Baba's the emperor sort. Exchanged his house with a Muslim's house in the village. They visit, Baba visits them too. Very friendly relations. They come to see their old house, my father goes to see his.

–Any other sisters and brothers?

–Both brothers are in the same line. One sister, she's in love with a schoolmaster, I'll get them married. She's the one who will inherit everything. You think any of us brothers will ever go back? I'd really like to marry and settle in the town, there's a huge difference between a town and a village.

–That sounds good.

–But it's out of the question. Once you join the line, there's no chance of settlement.

–But Dinu-babu got married.

–For how long? Those who came before us could have both line and home life. Our time is not like that. Take Bharat, he could have continued for at most another four or five years. Then he'd have had to stop and settle.

–Bharat wasn't in this line.

–You knew?

An explosive moment. They stared at each other. Then Tiger said, 'We're going back tomorrow. Bhabani-da is back in the town. We'll hold a meeting in the field by the station. The new MLA will attend. Ensuring peace, condemning police inaction, everything will be there.'

*

Everything was there. Bhabani-babu was there too. As soon as he stepped into the town streets, Tapan realized everyone knew everything. Even Shobuj was scared to look at him.

Bhabani-babu said, 'Did you know, the whole Bharat thing is being blamed on Dinu now?'

– How did that happen?

– Bharat had fought with Malay.

– Never mind. You paid me very little.

– Don't be obsessed with money, Tapan. Your time is coming. People are talking about Dinu. The byarakbaari needs to be shut down for some time. We need to clean up our image. Sudhin-babu, the new MLA, is a rabid dog. He was in the workers' unions earlier, now he's come to power.

Sudhin Senroy, reflected Tapan. Involved with the trade union movement for a long time. From '72 to '77, he hadn't lived in the town but in the slums. Maybe he would succeed in cleaning up the town. Ridding it of Bhabani-babu, Dinu-babu, Irani, Malay, Tapan, Tiger, the whole lot of them.

– It's not correct, what you're thinking. Everyone is a good man when they come to power. Then they change slowly.

– These people won't change.

– Everyone changes. They're all human, after all.

– Let's see.

–What's to see? Oh, by the way, why's that sister of yours moving around with Shyamal?

–I didn't know about it. But what if she is? How many boys do we have in the town like him?

–Do you know what you're saying? Shyamal's group holds meetings against us all the time. He's been to jail. And how much does he make anyway? Coaches school students, has his club, still Naxal-minded, can't you tell? Sudhin-babu is suspicious of them too.

–It was this government that let them all out.

–Doesn't mean you'll support them.

–No one at home talks to me. I'll ask around.

–Do. Dinu's overdoing things too.

*

Dinu-babu had indeed overdone things. His loyalty to the Congress was unalloyed. But Mohanlal's defeat, despite his every effort to the contrary, had been a tragic blow. Nothing like this had taken place from '52 to '77. And then Bhabani-babu's entry into the Sudhin-babu 'welcome committee' had been wholly beyond his comprehension.

–It's all going wrong, Irani.

–I can see.

–I hear they'll close down the byarakbaari.

–May I say something?

–Of course.

–You should get away.

–Who do I fear?

–At least for some time.

–No, I won't. And as long as I'm here, I'll support the Congress. Is it true, they're organizing a Kali Puja in the field by the station this year? I won't allow it. For thirty years now, we're the ones who . . . Everyone even calls it Dinu-Kali . . .

And thus, not over a political issue, but over a proposed Kali Puja, did Dinu-babu script his own exit. When Tapan heard about it afterwards, he realized Dinu-babu had read the writing on the wall. Why else did he attend the felicitation ceremony for Sudhin-babu, considering he hadn't even been invited?

*

When Sudhin-babu announced: I promise I will free the town from the terror of the antisocials, and in this task I will be helped by the power of the youth, then Dinu-babu did not join in the ensuing applause. For neither Bhabani-babu nor Tapan had deigned to acknowledge his presence.

Back at the byarakbaari, Dinu-babu drank a lot that night. Then he told Mashi, 'They'll take it out on all of you.'

–Are they going to shut us down?

–That they won't. Who wants to give up on a fixed income? But someone else will be in charge. I suspect it'll be Tapan. Malay thinks I'm an ass. Does he believe I don't know whose doormat he's using to scrape the mud off his shoes? How come he's not been around these last few days? Whenever you ask, they say he's unwell. No matter, you rise, you fall, that's the way of the world.

–What about our donation for your Kali Puja?

–I won't let go of the station field. But I'm not taking any more money from you, I've taken enough.

It was for possession of the field that Dinu pitched his final battle. Anticipating a split in their numbers over the location of the Kali Puja and expecting a significant amount of trouble as a result, the new puja committee had sought the help of the police.

–You're building the pandal, you're organizing a Jatra show, what trouble are you talking about?

–Dinu-babu will create trouble.

–No chance, he's gone absolutely quiet.

The stage had been constructed. The idol was yet to arrive. But the Jatra stage, the book stalls, the food stalls, those were all in place. The people were euphoric. Reduced to silence for years, now, after the elections, they were elated. The elaborate light displays and the songs on the loudspeakers had begun already, from the day before. A heavily financed celebration. The idol would be placed on its dais on the morning of the puja.

Sharp at nine that night, the skies turned red. The dais was on fire, the Jatra stage was burning. Bombs exploded, one after another. Everyone ran back home and slammed their doors shut in fear.

Dinu and Irani were on the spot, on a motorbike. As everything burned, Dinu hurled the remaining bombs here and there, and then rode away.

Tiger was with Tapan. Both wearing dark glasses. They knew Dinu would go to the byarakbaari. Malay was behind them.

'Don't get involved in the action,' said Tapan.

–There are two of them.

–Stop talking.

All the shops in the lane leading to the byarakbaari were closed. The windows of every room were shut. Tapan threw a brick at the street light.

Dinu slipped inside. This was his territory, everyone here knew him, he did not anticipate danger. Besides, he still had some of his people stationed here. What he didn't know was that they had all been compromised.

Tapan nudged Malay.

–Dinu-da?

–Malay, you?

Dinu got off his motorbike. Irani saw shadows moving in the darkness. He cried out, 'Dinu-da . . .'

Tapan's knife flew through the air and embedded itself in Irani's throat. Slashing it from right to left, Tapan then raised his arm in Dinu-babu's direction.

Dinu's hand was moving towards his pocket.

'Don't take a chance, Tapan,' yelled Malay.

Malay's words revealed everything to Dinu.

–Ah, it's Tapan . . .

Dinu couldn't finish. Tapan's knife plunged beneath the ribs to his left, emerged, plunged, emerged once more.

Tapan wiped the blade on Dinu's clothes.

Then he got back on his motorbike. Two motorbikes had entered, two left. On their way out, Malay hurled one bomb and Tiger, another.

*

No one knew who called the police, but their van arrived. The dead body was placed on the police-station veranda. Let the people come, let the people see, that the most notorious antisocial in the town was gone.

The infamy of the victim was matched by the ecstasy over his death. Bombs exploded frequently. 'Inter-gang antisocial violence results in deaths,' said the headlines.

'Has anything changed?' said Mashi at the byarakbaari. 'New government, so many meetings and processions, but those same bombs and goondas. One Dinu-babu has gone, another will come.'

Bhabani-babu went to meet Dinu-babu's wife and offer words of consolation.

–We may not be relatives by blood, but we're family still. How could I not be here in a crisis? But, Bouma. I warned Dinu so many times to be careful, would he listen? No. And that place he would frequent, that den of sin . . .

Dressed in her new widow's garb, Dinu-babu's wife glared belligerently at Bhabani-babu.

–I'll make sure there's no delay after the autopsy . . .

The defeated Congress candidate Mohanlal-babu swept in with his entourage.

–Don't worry, everything will be taken care of. But Boudi, you have to pay a visit to the police station.

–Why? To file a General Diary? What's the use? Better to wait for Manab, he'll do the last rites for his father. I'll do whatever he says. Please tell Bhabani-babu to leave, I can't take it any more.

Bhabani-babu refused to give up.

–Does Maya know?

'I moved the children to my parents' a long time ago thanks to their father's goings-on,' Dinu-babu's wife said angrily. 'My daughter's happily married in Begusarai. What will she come for, to see what, to hear what? You can go now. But let me tell you something, my husband chose the wrong path, that's why he died the way he did. I wouldn't wish such a death even on my enemies. But does that mean his killers are on the right path? They'll die the same way.'

–You're grieving now, Bouma, I won't say any more now.

–It's best you don't. I have my son Manab, after all.

'Don't talk to him that way, Boudi,' said Mohanlal after Bhabani-babu left, 'there'll be trouble.'

–Why, will he kill Manab too?

–Won't go so far.

–Thakurpo, maybe Manab shouldn't come. Stop him from coming. I'll do the last rites, it's allowed when there's been a calamity. It was an unnatural death, anyway. I'll do the rest of the rituals in Calcutta.

–What about the house?

–I'll sell everything. Who will protect me here? I've bought some land in Bidhannagar, I'll build a house there. Won't stay here any more. You'll have to make all the arrangements.

*

A sullen air descended on the town. No one except Mohanlal put garlands on the truck carrying Dinu-babu's corpse. No one knew if Irani had family anywhere. The police cremated him.

Dinu-babu's wife completed her husband's last rites and went away to Calcutta.

Mohanlal-babu bought Dinu-babu's house. Manab was a building contractor in Calcutta, he built the new house himself. 'Baba wasn't just any other man,' he told his mother, 'have you any idea how much business I get because I'm his son?'

And so Dinu-babu's name was wiped out from the town. Tapan's standing improved greatly in Bhabani-babu's eyes.

The town began to fear Tapan.

Even his parents were scared stiff of him now.

Reba alone maintained her disdain.

'Reba says she'll leave,' Tapan's mother told him.

–Where will she go?

–Ask her yourself.

–Where is she?

Reba came up to Tapan. No, there was no fear in her. There was something else. But Tapan couldn't tell what it was.

–Where will you go?

–Shyamal's got a job with a pharma company.

–What company?

–A small one.

–Where?

–The office is in Calcutta. He'll have to go on tours.

–Will you marry him?

–We've done a registered marriage already.

–So do the traditional wedding now.

–No, Shyamal says if I go, I have to leave everything behind. He doesn't want to have anything to do with anyone here. Not even visits.

–Such arrogance!

–I don't want it either, Dada.

–You, how dare you?

–What will you do, hit me? Go on then.

Tapan was deeply hurt. 'You really thought I'd hit you?'

–What else should I think?

–I'm your brother . . .

–I don't want you or Baba or Ma or anyone else. I've been eating my meals at someone else's house since I was twelve. Who looked after me then? I want a family, Dada, not money.

–So you don't want my money.

–I don't want anyone's money.

–Who's got the marriage papers?

–I do.

–When did you do the registry thing?

–The day Bharat died.

–I see.

–I want to live somewhere else, with honour. I feel choked here. If you stop me, I'll hang myself.

Tapan sighed.

–Why would you do such a thing?

–Don't you understand why Suku and Buku have left?

–I do. All right, do what you must to be happy, whether it's Calcutta, a rented place . . .

–People in slums have lives too.

–Shouldn't I talk to Shyamal?

–What for? I'm twenty-two, he's twenty-seven. Everyone else knew we were getting married, you're the only one who didn't.

–Have I been around to know? Tell Shyamal to be careful when he comes and goes, Bhabani-babu doesn't like him.

–He won't come back once he's gone.

–Don't leave together, everyone will find out. Reba, will it help if I go away?

–I'm leaving anyway.

Reba did leave, two days later. She didn't take any clothes or jewellery, walked out with her held head high.

'They'll set up a home of their own,' Tapan's mother said. 'I gave them two hundred out of my earnings.'

Reba's decision became a tremendous experience for Tapan. He felt he had grown up hating himself and his family even though they had lived under the same roof. He had never thought about his siblings. Although he had told his mother the day Bhabani-babu had first given him money, 'Get Reba back, Suku and Buku too.'

But he had begun to realize that money couldn't solve everything. He'd also begun to become a different person. Perhaps he had no choice but to surrender to that different becoming.

But the affluence ushered in by that different Tapan could not entice his siblings to change their lives. An elder brother who acts as a role model can make his sibling swell with pride. Not in Tapan's case.

Suku had left for Ranaghat. His radio-repair and electrical shop was small but thriving. Buku sold clothes imported from Bangladesh in Bongaon. Their mother had visited them both.

*

Reba had left. Shyamal must have asked her to wipe out her earlier identity. And well he might. Champak and Shyamal had both been released from jail, but Champak was murdered by Malay. Shyamal took over the press-workers' union that Champak had founded. And now Shyamal was leaving behind that same union?

'What else could he have done?' Tapan's mother said. 'People from Sudhin-babu's party are everywhere, the first thing they'll grab will be the unions.'

'Who's the new secretary?' Shyamal asked softly.

–Tirtha. One of Sudhin-babu's party boys. In the middle of all this, we're the one's who'll suffer. If Shyamal had been here . . .

–What would he have done?

–We nurses would have formed a union of our own.

–You'd never have joined it.

–Others would have benefited. And what do I have to do at home anyway? Even Reba has left now.

–Visit your sons.

–Can I say something, Tapan?

–What?

–Suku wants to expand his shop.

–What does Buku want?

–Wants to marry his business partner's daughter. Lives alone, has to cook his own meals now.

Tapan rubbed his temples.

–If they don't mind, let them tell me how much, I'll give the money.

–Why should they mind?

–They won't? Good. Ma, get them both married. You'll have somewhere to go. And find out the address from Shyamal's family, you can visit Reba too.

–You won't stop me?

–Why should I? Reba did no wrong, said no wrong either. And Shyamal's not like me—he's a human being.

Ma was silent.

–I can't help with your worries, Ma, I can at best give some money. Nothing more.

–Your father says . . .

–Don't talk to me about him. When did he ever think about anyone else? Why should I think of him now?

–True.

–Wife works as a maid in a hospital, daughter cooks for someone's family . . . All things considered, your other children have turned out all right, Ma.

In his head Tapan said, 'Thanks to you. Everything you did was right, everything I did was wrong.'

–Ma!

–What?

–Don't you feel like going away too?

–No. You'd have no one.

–Just for me?

–Four rooms, the house seems so empty now. Like it'll swallow me.

–You can live with your other sons. I'll send you money.

–No, Tapan. I worry for you.

–For me? I've never thought about you, but you think about me?

–I do. I couldn't do anything for you.

Tapan stares at his mother in surprise. A hard, wiry body, toughened by unrelenting hard work, an utterly ugly face, a broad band of vermilion in her fast thinning hair—this woman worried about him?

Tapan shook his head. He couldn't think of such things any more today. Things might have been different had his life been normal.

–If only your father had been a real man . . . you would have had a job by now.

A job! That was what Tapan had wanted from Bhabani-babu.

–Are you going out?

–I might. Listen, don't let anyone sleep in the front room. I'll sleep in the room at the back.

*

Tapan went out to buy cigarettes. He knew the shopkeeper. He was about to pay when the man said softly, 'Never mind.'

–Meaning?

–No need to pay.

Tapan realized it wasn't just the shopkeeper, everyone in town knew the truth. Dinu-babu was gone. Bhabani-babu had unfurled a new flag. Tapan was the new boss. He recalled that the boss and his men never paid for tea or cigarettes. They collected protection money from shopkeepers. They crushed the public underfoot.

Tapan felt as if the shopkeeper had suddenly slapped him.

'Take the money,' said Tapan. 'Let me know if anyone takes a packet and refuses to pay.'

With Dinu-babu gone, Tapan had obviously taken over. But that didn't mean he would move around town with his gang, collect protection money.

What he didn't know yet was that there would be another takeover in a few years. Those who had made their entrance under political banners would become bosses too. Tapan had no inkling of how they would terrorize the public, of the violent tyranny they would unleash. He had no idea that the revulsion for antisocials, the respect for political workers and the distinct line separating the two would all become blurred one day, that thousands of antisocials would infiltrate the lower rungs of political organizations.

The future cannot be seen, after all.

Tapan had identified himself as the most despicable of criminals. Anyone who murdered people on his leader's request was nothing but a hired killer.

He also knew he would never get out of this. 'None of us will die in our beds,' Dinu-babu used to say. Such was the line they were in.

TWO

'Meet me in Calcutta,' Bhabani-babu had said.

–The OC was saying there'll be a round of arrests.

–Naturally. To suppress the criminals. We're the ones who asked them to.

–But then . . .

–Doesn't concern you. Don't worry about it.

'You're out of their net and so am I, which criminals will they catch then?' Tapan was tempted to ask.

But he didn't. Not the right time, now was not the time.

–Heard about Dinu's case?

–Heard what?

–He threw bombs in a clash in Jagaddal, so they came and finished him off.

–That's not true.

–Dinu would have died one way or another. Don't worry about it. Keep your mind free, Tapan. You have to do these things, yes, but then you have to forget about them too. Now, to business.

–Tell me.

–We'll talk in Calcutta. But there's something I must tell you now. You weren't right to let Shyamal go.

–Shyamal's married Reba. Besides, he can't do his trade-union stuff here any more.

–That's true. Has he really married her?

–Yes, I've seen the papers.

–See what happens. Your sister . . .

Tapan realized that it wasn't safe to be candid with Bhabani-babu. 'I've warned him,' he said, 'he won't dare come back.'

–Your sister could have married far better.

–Since childhood they've been . . .

–I see, love? Very good, love is very good.

Bhabani-babu smiled. Sometimes he smiled like this. Or said something completely imaginary, which he himself believed only for that moment. Now he said, 'Who else will live the life of a bachelor like me? I'd brought home a goddess, a fire took her away. I wasn't old, I could have married again. Men can marry whenever they wish. I could have if I'd wanted. But I thought it over, it was impossible. You never saw her.'

–I did when I was a child. On her way to the Durga Puja. She'd give money for our Saraswati Puja too.

–Devoted to the gods. No surprise, she was from such an illustrious family, but look whom she married.

–Yes.

–Anyway, that's why I went into the public line. It seems Mohanlal is the one who bought Dinu's house.

–I heard.

–So many years they lived there, all gone now. Never mind. I told Dinu so many times, tried so hard to make him understand.

Tiger, Malay and Tapan were silent. What could they say?

–Hirak has good prospects. If he's trained properly . . .

–As you say.

–We'll talk in Calcutta. Here we'll have to split the line if we're to carry on. New era, we need new rules. I'll explain everything. Heard about Dinu's wife, by the way? She's become quite the Rani Rashmoni.

–How do you mean?

–She gave two–four–five thousand each to her cook and maid and doorman and driver. Said they were very faithful, they'd protected her.

–Where are they?

–All disappeared. Made to disappear, rather. They knew about Dinu's exploits, after all.

Tapan waited.

–You don't look too happy. Feeling bad?

–No, I've got a headache.

–OK, then, come with Tiger the day after tomorrow. Tiger is going anyway to get the car serviced.

–When?

–Come in the morning. Have lunch with me. You think your boudi will let you go without eating? Not her.

Tapan went out. No one knew where Bhabani-babu's brothers lived. Tiger had said that Renu-boudi, for whom Bhabani-babu bought a house in Bhabanipur in Calcutta, used to be a sex worker. Bhabani-babu picked her up from a brothel, kept her for a long time. They had two daughters too, Bhabani-babu had himself arranged their marriages. There was no doubt that they would inherit his riches.

'How do you know so much?' Tapan had asked.

–Just like he keeps track of everything I do, I keep track of everything he does. It's called insurance. He knows I know every-thing about him. That's the insurance. Someone who knows can tell others too. He won't try to make another Bharat out of a person like that. Times are bad, Dada, everyone keeps track of everyone else.

–Why are you telling me this?

–There's something I want to beg you for.

–What are you saying?

–Will you teach me how to use a knife?

–Tiger!

–What?

–You're a guns man.

–Yes, but the knife's far better.

–I used to accompany Rohanlal at one time. He would show his knife-throwing skills everywhere from here to Sealdah. His daughter stood against a board, he threw knives all around her.

–Did you show the trick too?

–No, I learnt it.

In his head Tapan said, 'I'm showing my tricks now.'

–Bhabani-da says you're an all-rounder. You can fire guns too, everything.

–If you have to be in this line, Tiger . . . Besides, I've been a goonda on the streets of this town since my childhood.

–I know everything. Anyway, remember what I said.

–Yes, plenty of time.

–You move about without a bodyguard.

–Irani was Dinu-babu's bodyguard.

–It's all fate. But you can avoid danger if you're cautious. Think of how many attempts the Naxals made on Bhabani-da's life.

–You're right. I'd better go now.

Could he count on being safe if he was cautious? Who could tell where danger was lurking. Today, because Reba had left suddenly, Tapan was reminded of Shyamal, of Champak. Police brutality in jail had fractured Champak's shoulder. No hospital, no treatment. His left arm became useless, hung limp. Even after that, Champak had organized the press-workers' union. They went on strike, demanding a ten-rupee daily wage.

It was Malay who killed Champak on his way back home.

A small but extremely reverential funeral procession had set out with Champak's body, draped in red cloth. The workers of eleven presses, small and big, had joined in. Shyamal and Sourav had been there too. Tapan had watched from a distance. Among the young political workers who had been arrested and jailed earlier, Kajal was murdered in North Bengal around the same time. His family left town. His sister Gauri had been in prison too, she was believed to be teaching in a college in Calcutta now.

Swati was supposed to have married Champak. She married Sourav later. Both of them had set up a small advertising agency in Calcutta.

That left Shyamal. Now he had left too.

Why was Tapan thinking of them? Why should a knife-for-hire, a killer-for-hire, think of them at all? That Shyamal had married Reba even after all this was a surprise. Maybe Reba would be saved, make herself a different life, a healthy existence.

*

Back home, Tapan's mother was waiting for him, with his dinner.

–Just some vegetables tonight, will it do?

–Do for whom, me? Of course it will. Don't stay up, Ma, go to bed.

He would have to leave home. It wouldn't be right to live here and keep his mother in a constant state of anxiety. Once Tapan had left, she would definitely be able to build relationships with her other sons.

The room in which Tapan slept that night used to be Reba's. Spick and span. Textbooks on history, geography and English grammar lined the shelves.

–Did Reba read these books?

–She did. Never went to school, but she meant to study at home and sit for the exams.

–Shyamal will make sure she does.

–It was because he encouraged her that . . .

–What about all these books on tailoring?

–She was learning to sew. She knows how to cut and measure blouses. I can earn if we can get a sewing machine, she would say. I'd say the same thing.

Tapan knew none of this.

–Reba used to say this?

–Why not? From her childhood she's seen me working hard. If I'd been a little better educated, I could even have become a nurse. What's better than a woman working to support herself? I've looked after so many patients.

Tapan used to have a low opinion of the work his mother did. He had no idea she was so proud of it.

– Do you know how to run a sewing machine?

– How would I know? I've long wanted to buy one, couldn't afford it. Not at the right time. Life is nearly over now. I can't even see clearly any more.

– Get your eyes checked at Ashish-babu's, Ma.

– He's too big a doctor for me. Maybe at the hospital . . .

– They don't have the machines at the hospital.

– All right, I'll go to him.

– What else do you wish for?

– Nothing, Tapan. They'll . . . be all right, I know. I want you to be all right too.

– I'll be all right, Ma.

Tapan would clearly have to leave home. If only for his mother to spend her last days in peace.

– Tapan.

– What?

– What if you could start a business or something . . .

– Too late for that, Ma. I'm too far down the wrong path. Don't ask me any questions.

*

When Tapan got into the car the next day, he realized he commanded a new respect from Tiger now. There was a constant 'Want some tea, Tapan-da? Want a glass of water?' all the way to Calcutta.

A three-storeyed building on Gopal Banerjee Road in Bhabanipur. A solid old-fashioned construction, with a tiled roof over the first-floor veranda. A small garden caught the eye as soon as the front gate swung open. A doorman at the entrance, and a collapsible gate protecting the veranda. 'Powerful alarm system,' said Tiger in an undertone. 'If they press the button upstairs, a bell rings in every room. He has to be careful, impossible to live otherwise.'

There were bodyguards at the gate and on the veranda. The room into which Tapan and Tiger were ushered in had iron mesh and blue glass at the windows. A huge room, with a table and chairs in the corner, several sofas. 'Bhabani-da's own chair is upstairs,' said Tiger.

Bhabani-babu came down, his slippers flapping loudly on the stairs. 'Why are you sitting here?' he said. 'Come upstairs. The first floor is mine. Your boudi is on the second floor.'

The first floor was done up the same way. But with another collapsible gate at the entrance. And rows of lockers built into the walls.

–What do you think, Tapan?

–Very nice.

–Destiny, it's all destiny. As they say, a gambler's purse knows no locks. The owner of this property went bankrupt at the races.

Thirty years ago, he mortgaged this three-storeyed building on these four kathas of land to me. He could never pay back the loan—his horses' tails swished away two houses in Calcutta and his entire film business. You lose as quickly as you gain in this world.

–So, tell me.

–All in good time, come see my garden first. You can see it from the veranda. Hibiscus, marigold, sweet pea, rose balsam, oleander, jasmine, name it and I've got it. The thakur-ghar is on the roof, where your boudi does her puja. She's installed Lakshmi–Janardhan idols there. These flowers are all for her rites and rituals. In my father's time, we used to have a grand Durga Puja in the town house, but now . . . Ah, here she is.

Boudi entered, followed by two maids bearing plates of food. Tiger had said she used to be a sex worker, but Tapan felt she might have been an actress. Fair-skinned and plump, a body soft as butter, dressed in a white silk sari, covered in jewellery. Plucked eyebrows, dyed hair.

–Please, have a little something.

Luchi and a vegetable curry, payesh, sweets.

–So much!

All offered to my gods first. Lunch will be vegetarian too, no meat or fish enters this house. Thakurpo eats whatever he wants but outside. Eat up, Tarak. I don't know the other gentleman's name.

–This is Tapan.

–So handsome! I wish I could have you as my son-in-law. But then, I have only the two girls, and their husbands are princes both. I'll show you their photos.

'Go on, eat,' said Bhabani-babu, 'there's work to be done.'

–What about you?

–I've eaten in the morning, with Sudhin-babu . . .

–Some more luchis for you?

–No please, no more for me.

–When Thakurpo was your age, he could . . .

–No one eats so much these days. Have *you* eaten?

–Me? Now? Do I have anything but milk and michhri in the morning? Something light in the afternoon. Look where eating's got me. My daughter took me to Mussoorie, I could barely walk.

'Try yoga,' said Bhabani-babu.

–Please! Yoga at this age. I'm prone to putting on weight, that's all. What's the use of trying to prevent it?

–Do some work, stay active.

–Oh god! Never done housework in my life, can't start now. I'm quite active, I go out all the time, go to the movies, can't do that at home, can I? You're the one who wants to work, go ahead. Let me be.

Tapan felt he knew her from somewhere, but he couldn't quite recall.

–I'd better go, you have work to talk about. Listen. It's all vegetarian food here, will you find it hard?

–Of course not, why should I?

–You've eaten here often enough, Tarak, I'm asking him.

–No, no, not at all.

–So handsome. Do you have a family?

'Can you leave us now?' Bhabani-babu said. 'We have work to do, work to talk about.'

–Naturally. What does a man have in life besides work?

Bhabani-babu's Renu-boudi slowly swayed her way out. Tapan remembered. Bhabani-babu used to send his cars to Tiger's brother-in-law's garage, so they could be hired out. That's where he'd seen her one day. Sitting in a car. Wearing sunglasses.

–Shut the door, Tiger. I have to talk to Tapan. Why so serious, Tapan?

–When was I a cheerful chap, Bhabani-da?

Tiger had instructed Tapan to say Bhabani-*da*. Bhabani-babu liked to be addressed as Dada. Tiger had also said, 'He's an expert at twisting words, so be very careful what you say to him.' It was because Dinu-babu didn't know how to twist words that he'd got into trouble.

Tapan couldn't tell what he could do to appear completely trustworthy to Bhabani-babu. He was no good at flattery. And considering Tapan had murdered someone at Bhabani-babu's behest, how could they be expected to trust each other? It was unrealistic.

–Do you have any ideas, Tapan?

–What ideas should I have?

–What do you mean? You're the young generation, you should be having new ideas. We're old now, has-beens.

–You have so much more experience.

–We have to be very careful now. New government . . .

–May I ask something?

–Do.

–Sudhin-babu and his people have a different politics from ours. They used to win the union elections. People supported them wholeheartedly, you can see it on the streets. Why will they support our, or rather your, programme? After all, they defeated your party and then came to power. I can see how happy the common man is with them.

Bhabani-babu's eyes softened with pity.

–You may be in politics, but you haven't understood the game.

–I'm not in politics Bhabani-da, that was Champak.

–Eliminated.

–Kajal was in politics too.

–Also eliminated. Never mind all that, let's get down to business. I was against them, yes, but I've realized my mistake now.

–Will they accept it?

–They're still straightforward people, how will they see through us? They aren't experienced, don't understand our tactics. They want to see who supports them and who doesn't.

–Then you . . . ?

–I'm their supporter too.

–How do you want to use us or me now? I'm asking you to show me the way.

–We have to be careful. It's true Sudhin-babu has been elected, but Laltu Basu also commanded respect in the trade union. It was he who used to stand for the elections earlier. Whether he won or not, he'd get many votes. Let me tell you, these two will continue to fight for power.

–That's their business.

–It would have been difficult for us to function if they had been united. It helps us if there's conflict between them.

–Will everything continue as before?

–What do you think will stop? Ramadhari Sahay will remain in the Congress union. Sudhin-babu can't be a union leader now. Laltu-babu will do what he can.

–And you?

–I'll be as I was. I'm not getting involved with Laltu-babu's union right now. Later, I'll definitely become an advisor. I have some experience in labour matters, after all.

Yes, the experience of sending in strike breakers or blacklegs once the strike was declared illegal. Bhabani-babu worked in the background, however, and it was always the mill owner who gained.

–We need new ideas, Tapan. Nylon thread is about to come into the market, how long do you suppose jute will be in demand? I'm telling you now, bad days are lying in wait for the mills, sooner or later they will be hit. Doesn't matter who runs the government, the bureaucrats will do all the work. You think they will start doing good for the poor overnight? Hah!

–What are you saying? These are industrial areas.

–Power, we need electricity. Workers cannot be incited. Only then will the mill owners operate their factories. They don't run their businesses so that people can get enough to eat—they run them to make profits. Don't you remember how many of them wound up their factories out of fear of the Naxals?

–What's to be done, then?

–Some things will go well, some not so well. You needn't involve yourself with politics. Dinu's gone, you're the boss now. Keep that in mind.

–But you're there . . .

–I'll always be in the background. When Dinu was there, everyone saw him, no one saw me. Besides, I'm going to spend more time in Calcutta now. All the political moves will be made in Calcutta, it's best I bide my time here now.

This was true. Dinu-babu used to be visible, Dinu-babu was the face. Dinu was a criminal, Dinu was a murderer who celebrated Kali Puja with everyone. Dinu visited the byarakbaari, Dinu drank every night before going home. Dinu made children do military drills on Netaji's birthday. Dinu patronized goondas. Dinu took the town's football team to watch the professional matches in Calcutta. Dinu wasn't faceless, he was visible, a man of flesh and blood.

And because he was flesh and blood, his shadow was visible too. The shadow always clings to the body. Irani was Dinu's shadow, he was visible too. He too could be seen. One day, both were found slumped on the ground. Covered in blood. Everyone saw. Dinu had no front, only a face.

Bhabani-babu would always remain behind the scenes. He was faceless, had no shadow. He created his own shadow, made it fall everywhere. His shadow was omnipresent.

Bhabani-babu followed the laws of physics.

Sudhin-babu and Laltu-babu used to be his opponents. Red-flag party. Ramadhari Sahay was his front, a leader in the Congress union.

Today Bhabani-babu was a supporter of Sudhin-babu's party. But Ramadhari would remain in the picture. Bhabani-babu didn't want unity among them, not just yet. Maybe one day he would ask the leaders to come to an understanding. But he would remain in the background. Let the workers die if they had to.

But it wasn't time for this, not yet.

Now what role would Tapan play in implementing Bhabani-babu's plan?

–What are you thinking of, Tapan?

–Nothing important.

–Let me do the thinking. You're meant for action, stick to it.

–Dinu-babu did the same thing.

–Oho, why must you think of him now? He had no control over his moral character. Or would he have visited the byarak-baari despite a wife like that at home? You won't find another brahmachari like me. Committed to celibacy. Wife died, never remarried.

–You set your own standards, Bhabani-da.

–So what are you worrying about?

–What should I do?

–Work out the plan. Tiger! How many hooch dens in operation right now?

–Sixteen.

–How are the takings from the Dalit slum?

–Pretty good.

–Close down six. Bring it down to ten. People will see six dens being shut down, Tapan, they won't mind the other ten. Oh yes, take a large group along when you go. Take a loudspeaker, tell the people it was Bharat Bansphor's dream to clear these dens from the Dalit slum, and now we're fulfilling his dream. In time, we'll shut down the others too. The police will pick them up. Same with the gambling. Bharat is gone. If you introduce the young men in the neighbourhood to drinking and gambling, they'll take to it, all of them. And they will become useless. It's not a good idea for all these boys to go astray. Just because we can't give them jobs, does it mean we'll make them worthless? Not that there aren't talented boys among them. See who you can get. That leaves the byarakbaari. Let Tiger take care of it.

–So it stays?

Bhabani-babu leant closer to Tapan.

–What are you saying, Tapan? Nine or ten girls there, where will they go? They'll be torn apart if we throw them out. How will they survive? Helpless women, where will they go? That's not ethical.

–Not nine or ten, Bhabani-da, more like thirty.

–Same thing. They get protection here. You may have noticed, a tailoring school's been set up. So they can pick up some skills and change their lives. Not that any of them wants to. They've discovered ways to make life tastier. Seen the school?

–I don't know, I've never been in there.

–And some shops downstairs . . .

–Yes, liquor shops . . .

–No point being a moralist, Tapan. You could say the whole thing is wrong, but you and I saying so doesn't make it wrong. This is how it is, all over the country, all over the world. Besides, let me say this straight out, I won't abandon those who joined the youth team on my personal assurance. You have to keep them on your side. What you don't understand is they'll prove useful one day.

–Tiger will take care of it.

–You bet he will. Sit tight. But keep an eye on everything. You have Bomba, you have Thanu, you have Rongeen, you have Malay. But if they come under fire, you'll be the one to take care of it all. Now, what will you do officially? You need a front.

–Yes, of course.

But what would be credible? The town knew Tapan only too well already. Who would trust someone whom the OC treated to tea and addressed as 'Tapan-babu'? Imagine the police being deferential to a man who'd done three murders in the very heart of town. Tapan could be a shopkeeper or start his own business— everyone would know it was only a front. Tapan was, in truth, a killer-for-hire, a murderer.

–Any ideas?

–I don't really know any line of work . . .

–Become a contractor.

–For what?

–Real estate . . . buildings . . . land development.

–Where will I set up my office?

–My house is too far. Start a partnership with Mohanlal . . . in Dinu's outhouse . . .

–Where's my capital?

–Ten for Mohanlal, six for you. I'll invest. As will Shuku-babu. He knows a bit about this land business. Expert at wriggling out of court cases. Let Malay, Thanu and Rabi be with you. Give them each a share. Say, this land business brings in high profits. Make sure you give them some before you enjoy the rest. I'll be owed a cut, but I won't take it. Because I'm the one who will develop the land, construct the houses.

–But Mohanlal-babu is . . .

–Congress? So what? We need to keep our secret alliances intact. Who knows, what if they return to power? Plus, don't forget, his brother Nandalal is the chairman of the municipality.

–Will this work?

Bhabani-babu turned into a god. He made a prediction which became a reality over the next eight years.

–It's the only business that will work. People have to live somewhere, don't they? I'll get your company to buy ten lakhs worth of property. In ten years, it'll be worth a crore. Calcutta won't be able to hold everyone. It will spit them out. People will look for property everywhere. You can't tell yet, but the days of living in houses are ending. Everyone will buy flats. I saw it in Bombay.

–I have something to say too.

–Go on. Don't hold anything back.

–I want a place of my own to live in.

–Live in the outhouse for now. In no more than three years' time, you'll find you've built your own house.

–I won't have anything to do with the byarakbaari.

–Not as a rule, but it's a safe house. What if you have to take shelter in the town, will you find a safer place? And Tapan! You're young, hot-blooded, and don't forget that you've been in action . . .

–Action? Me?

–I see. So you assume action is only what the Naxals do? That's not correct, what you do is action too.

–No. Are Champak and I the same? Champak never killed anyone, but he was murdered.

–And you have murdered, but no one can touch you now.

–Anyway. Go on.

–I know, I know, you're sympathetic to their cause. Or would you have agreed to your sister marrying Shyamal? I don't mind. As I was saying, whatever you have done was on my instructions. You're the boss now. You'll ensure protection for our boys in the town. Make sure everyone pays the police their share. Make sure there's no unnecessary violence.

–How? Will you give me a free hand?

–In what sense? I didn't go in for higher education, my boy. I had the chance. Not that it ever mattered. But I understand straight talk, not twisted words.

–I'm talking straight. Some things will have to be stopped. This business of taking things from shops without paying, collecting protection money, harassing peddlers, groping women on the streets . . . this kind of behaviour makes enemies out of the public. All this has become rampant.

–That's very good, Tapan. You sound like a man who understands politics perfectly. I'm giving you a free hand. Especially molesting women—no, no, all that must stop. Everyone will praise us. Even Sudhin-babu will realize we want to change our ways.

–It's become a habit.

–Break the habit. And stay clean yourself. Once upon a time, Dinu had vowed to remove prostitution from the town, to not touch alcohol himself nor let others touch it. Did he succeed?

–We always saw him drinking.

–You're young, you haven't seen Dinu's mother. A spirited woman. She had a weakness for her younger son. Lived with him. When Dinu went bad, his wife used to abuse her: You spoilt him so much you've ruined him. She had the right to say it, she came from quite a rich family. Her father gave her a gold tiara for her wedding. When all of his mother's pleas couldn't make Dinu change his mind, she said: I don't want to see an evil son's face, and went off to live with her older son. That son had already built himself a house in Sodepur. Had a roaring legal practice. But his wife gave the mother-in-law a very hard time. The poor old woman was abused to death.

Bhabani-babu grew thoughtful.

–Dinu was a big name hereabouts. When he lost a hand making bombs, all the top leaders visited him. But when he died, no one came.

Bhabani-babu's manner of speaking suggested that Dinu-babu died a natural death, that Tapan hadn't murdered him. Tapan's blood slowly began to boil. Was Bhabani-babu baiting him, testing him?

–Want to smoke? Go ahead.

–No, I don't smoke much.

–Anyway, you've been faithful. I'm not ungrateful either. You will get your money. You can bring your brothers in too, if you like.

Don't even think of them, Tapan thought, they've moved away, let them be safe. But if he said it out loud, then Bhabani-babu would know that of late Tapan had grown quite anxious about his siblings.

–No need, I have no relations with them anyway. I left home so long ago.

–I know. But your mother visits them.

–That's why I want to move out.

–Are you thinking of getting married?

–Who, me?

Smiling faintly, Tapan shook his head.

–You're becoming depressed, Tapan. Getting married is good. Having someone of your own is good. Loneliness is not . . .

What loneliness? He was no longer the Tapan he'd been eight years ago. Reba's marriage had made him think for the first time about his family, his mother, his brothers, all of them. He was now desperate that his shadow not fall on their lives.

–Force those goondas out of town. That Shobuj . . .

–Shobuj is no threat, Bhabani-da.

–Don't forget whose brother he is.

–I'll take care of it.

What would Tapan take care of? Shobuj had been a criminal since his childhood. He would cut classes, steal money from home. It was hard to believe he was Shyamal's brother. Why should Tapan drive him out? Tapan realized that Bhabani-babu wanted to make a name for himself by taking revenge on the powerless, on people like Shobuj.

–Do you know where Shyamal is?

–I don't. Don't want to know either.

–The Naxals will rise again unless you rein them in firmly. It's a terrible disease.

Let them come, Tapan reflected. Let them make the Bhabanis tremble in terror.

–If you act wisely, you can make serious money in this line that I've given you. The money is in land right now, you see? And yes, you have to look happier.

–Yes.

–Why are you so worried? When I was your age . . .

–I'll take care of it.

–Do you have a bank account?

–No.

–What use is it anyway? Leave the business management to Mohan-babu. The company will be registered in both your names. Open an account for now, later you'll see it's better to keep your money in a safe in your room.

Tapan smiled.

–I'll learn. Didn't have any money, didn't know any of this. If I make money, I'll also learn how to keep it safe. But can you tell me something?

–What?

–Bharat, Dinu-babu, Irani, why isn't the police investigating their murders?

The look in Bhabani-babu's eyes changed.

–The murderers couldn't be caught. They're absconding. The case is open. They could always be caught, the police could always say they hadn't found them earlier. If you watch your step, the case will remain under wraps. Dinu's wife could have tried, but Mohanlal didn't encourage her. She has a son, she was afraid. As for Irani, who's going to push his case?

–That's true.

–Don't let your thoughts run wild. They won't write anything in the papers just yet. But who knows what will happen afterwards.

Tapan sighed.

–No, why should I think such thoughts.

–It's my job to think, you concentrate on the action. Now relax. I'll go for my bath. You can leave after lunch. You want to use the bathroom, don't you, go out to the veranda, it's on the right.

Bhabani-babu left. Finally, Tiger stirred. How strange, he had neither spoken nor moved all this while.

'I told you so many times, be careful of what you say,' he told Tapan, 'but you didn't listen.'

–I'll learn, Tiger.

–Do you hate the byarakbaari so much?

–There are some things I can do, and some that I can't.

–Good news for me, actually.

–That was what you wanted.

–Business is business, boss. But then, you've got to the level that counts. If you take my advice, you'll keep a gun with yourself too. I'll tell you more on the way back.

Tapan went to the bathroom, splashed some water on his face. He felt like a trapped animal. When had Bhabani-babu bought him? When?

Had he really had a childhood? Had he really flown kites made by Bharat's father Dhanu? Had he ever been a volunteer during the Durga Puja celebrations? Was it he who had recited poetry on stage, alongside Champak, Shyamal and Sourav? That was all part of someone else's life.

Rows of buildings could be seen through the bathroom window, a concrete jungle. Calcutta was a jungle, and somewhere in it were Reba and Shyamal.

He didn't want to know where. Just let them be happy.

Shyamal had made the right choice. Why should he want to have anything to do with Tapan, whose name was synonymous with terror? Had Shyamal done the things that Tapan had done, and if he had wanted to marry Shyamal's sister, he would have made the same demand as Shyamal.

Tapan came out of the bathroom.

'Sit down, they'll send for us.' said Tiger.

Tapan leafed through the newspapers. A Bengali daily, a film tabloid, a telephone directory too.

'There's a phone here, but it's unlisted,' said Tiger. 'Renu-boudi has one too, that's in the directory. Seen what the house is like? Jaipur marble everywhere. All these doors and windows, this is what a house should be like. It's even better done up upstairs.'

They had to go to the next room for lunch. A marble table, gleaming bell-metal plates surrounded by bowls.

–Nothing special, just what I serve my gods.

–Aren't you eating?

–I eat later.

'She bathes constantly,' said Bhabani-babu, 'four times a day. And then won't eat this, won't eat that.'

–What to do? A congenital tendency towards fatness. If I'm greedy about food, I'll die.

Pulao, white rice, luchis, moong dal, five kinds of fried vegetables, mocha chops, chhana curry, potato curry, chutney, kheer, enormous sweets.

Benevolently, the woman said, 'Cooked in pure ghee and oil. Eat without fear.'

Bhabani-babu wolfed it all down. 'Without some meat or fish . . .' he said. 'Can I have two more chops, please.'

–I cooked everything myself. Didn't know anything about it at first. Then with the help of recipe books . . .

They returned to the drawing room after lunch. Bhabani-babu unlocked a safe and took out a large envelope.

–There's a full ten thousand in there. Put it in the bank.

*

On the way back, Tiger said, 'He brought up Shyamal to test you. I've seen him long enough to know. I know him only too well.'

–What do I know about Shyamal?

–You don't, but he doesn't believe you. Your sister's a very good girl, boss, I've passed by her on the streets.

–Did you ever talk to her?

–My god! Me, talk to *your* sister? Where are they, though?

–I don't know. And Tiger, I don't want to hear anything about my home or family, I have nothing to do with them. I live in the same house, but that's not for long either.

–You'll have your own house, I'm sure.

–Who knows. Tell me, you get good money too, then why don't you build a house for yourself? And, for that matter, why do you drink so much?

Tiger shrugged and gestured helplessly with his hands.

–The money. Some of it I've put into investments, the rest I blow up. A house! My father's built a house, my parents live in it. When my sister's married, her husband will come and live there too. All three of us brothers work in this line. My parents know everything, but tell everyone their sons are 'in business'.

–Does your father work?

–Pesticides dealer. Sometimes I think of marrying, building a house, settling down. But it's too late. Everything is temporary when you're in this line. Nothing can be permanent. What I want to do now is buy a heavy truck. Transport goods from Bengal to Punjab, Punjab to Madhya Pradesh. Good business. Besides, I've been told by an astrologer, there's some hazard waiting for me when I turn forty.

–Sounds like a plan.

–But where's the money for it? Look at Bhabani-da, how well he's doing for himself. His wife died, but he got a new lease of life. The one you saw, she's been with him a long time, she's become permanent. Even though she calls him Thakurpo. And her daughters, they know perfectly well he's their father, but they act coy and call him Kaka. Take my word for it, Bhabani-da will die peacefully in his own bed.

Tapan smiled.

–And we?

–We'll be slaughtered. Any doubt about it? Gang wars will break out among ourselves, boss. You took out Dinu-babu, now you're the boss. Anyway, best to follow Bhabani-da's instructions. Tirtha and the rest of them don't trust anyone. Let it go on this way for now. He will certainly double-cross us one day.

–We'll see. Tirtha is stubborn, but useful too.

–The police have dossiers on all of us, you, me, Malay. When the time is right, Bhabani-da will hand us over to them without a second thought.

–Let's see.

–Best not to ask so directly for things like you just did. Maybe you don't care much for your life.

–Even if I do, doesn't mean my life is my own.

–You'll become popular, boss. If you can put an end to the hooliganism and protection money . . .

–That's essential, Tiger. Not for Bhabani-babu but for us. It's a tactical error to have the whole town angry with us. You never know when we might need shelter. We need to do at least some things that the people approve of.

–Might be true. But it's a matter of habit.

–I'll change habits. And you must stop picking up women around the town.

–Whatever each of us is good at. But I don't have to pick up women, they come on their own.

–Remember what I said.

–You're beginning to sound like a boss.

Tapan had never wanted to be a boss. Yet he kept doing whatever was necessary to become one.

THREE

Tapan became the boss.

Giving his mother some money, he said, 'Your son wants to expand his shop or something, will this help a little?'

–What do you mean a little? It will help a lot.

It should have. Money was still worth something then. With the Left Front coming to power, there was a surge in enthusiasm among the ordinary people. Tapan's mother looked quite pleased when she got the money. Did she not know the source?

Tapan's situation was like the bandit Ratnakar's. Before he was transformed into Valmiki, his family had told him: It's your responsibility to look after us, we don't want to know how you'll do it.

–Suku will take the money, I hope.

–He will. There's no one else giving him any either.

–Let him get the shop going properly. He'd talked of getting married, let him. I couldn't do anything for them. But if they can stand on their own two feet, there's nothing as good as that.

Tapan's mother sighed.

–Yes, they know how to live frugally. The girl's good too, a homebody. Let them live in peace. It needs a husband and wife to understand each other.

A small shop, a small house. A kerosene stove, simple arrangements for cooking. Suku had the extraordinary capacity to be happy with nothing more than this and that quiet girl for a wife.

A simple life, a life that ran along a straight line. Like Bharat's sister Chameli's home. Sparkling clean, the kitchen utensils stashed away beneath the bed propped up on bricks. Chameli was thin, petite. But how happy she was with her life, with her husband and her children.

But not any more, surely. Her little hovel had Bharat's blood-stains all over it now. Tapan had robbed them of their happiness and peace.

Perhaps Bharat hadn't wanted any more happiness either. Nor had Reba and Shyamal. Tapan hadn't realized how tranquil life could be even with such simple things.

Tapan's mother would be so delighted when a patient's family gave her a sari and some money at the hospital. But it made Tapan furious. How happy she would be if his father managed to come home without drinking. A piece of fish on the plate, and how Suku and Buku's faces would light up.

He hadn't understood the value of these things. Now that he had, there was no way of going back. Would he ever be able to wipe away the marks of all his mistakes?

'Reba and Shyamal are well,' said Tapan's mother. 'They're in Calcutta ...'

Tapan seemed to grow afraid.

–Don't tell me, Ma, don't tell me where they live. And don't mention them in the town. You don't know, Ma, Bhabani-da is furious with Shyamal. Don't tell me, I don't want to know. Just tell me they're all right.

Tapan's mother fell silent.

–I won't live here any more either, Ma.

–Where will you live?

–In the town. But elsewhere.

–Will living at home mean ...

–It's not a good idea. I ... I'll come by, I'll take care of you. Don't worry. I'm making money. Get your eyes checked, get a pair of glasses. Open a bank account, it's not safe to keep money at home.

–Are you in danger, Tapan?

Tapan glanced at his mother. There was no danger at the moment, but as his name became more and more synonymous with terror, there would be danger for his parents. How was he to explain this complex calculation to his mother? She wouldn't understand.

–No, Ma, I'm not in any danger. But everyone thinks I have no real relationship with my family. It's best they think so. No one will connect any of you with anything I do.

–Can't you . . . go away somewhere?

–Where will I run to, from myself? Stop worrying about me.

–That's easy for you to say.

Tapan couldn't understand her at all. Why couldn't he get his mother within his reach? He felt like telling her, 'Have I ever worried about you? Why should you worry about me now?'

What he said was, 'What's the use of worrying when it won't serve any purpose. Listen, I want you to look for a maid. You don't have to do everything yourself any more.'

–All right.

–Tell Suku. I'll send money as and when I get some, I'll send more. Buku too.

*

Everyone in the town had taken note of Tapan becoming the boss. Laltu-babu represented Sudhin-babu as the local political leader. The senior leaders were not always available, the local leaders were the junction station for both the upper and lower echelons.

Laltu-babu's home doubled up as the office. Back then, at least. Ten years later, there was a new office building. Back then, the first unofficial meeting took place at Laltu-babu's.

Tirtha, Abhik, Babul and Somjit were the leaders among the younger lot. Tirtha was slightly older, he'd been in the same class as Champak, Tapan and Shyamal in school. Calm and composed, he always thought carefully before he spoke. Even when he spoke of simple things, he uttered the words slowly and in a deep voice. Abhik felt that Tirtha possessed all the qualities required of a leader. Babul was a hard worker. He had no initiative, but would put his heart and soul into whatever he was asked to do. Somjit was cheerful, sweet-tempered. A pensive young man, more interested in cultural matters. He played the mouth organ marvellously.

Tirtha said, 'It will be impossible to free the town of these criminal types, Laltu-da. Dinu-babu may be gone, but now we have Tapan.'

Abhik was used to being direct. He said, 'It was Bhabani-babu who propped up Dinu-babu.'

'What are you trying to say?' said Laltu-babu.

–How is it that Bhabani-babu helped Sudhin-da's campaign during the elections? Why? And why for that matter did we accept his help?

–People do change, after all. Bhabani had realized his mistake.

–He's going into business with Mohanlal.

–Oppose them politically. Expand the organization, grow stronger. Most industrialists in this state used to vote for the Congress. Will this state ever see economic development if we turn everyone into enemies and exclude them?

–But to work with murderers and criminals?

–As long as I'm alive, I'll never ask you to work with murderers and criminals. None of you is an antisocial. If you try to oppose them at this moment, violence will break out in town again.

–Why don't you force the police to take action?

Somjit raised a placatory hand.

–Slow down, my friend, slow down. Nothing will change overnight. The police take bribes, they obey the corrupt and the criminals, the political leaders. You think they'll take action just because we tell them to? They didn't in Champak-da's case, they didn't in Bharat's either.

–Why talk about Champak?

–He wasn't working with the Naxals when he came out of jail. We should have demanded an investigation, just as we did for Bharat.

–Who do you think killed Champak?

'We're digressing,' said Tirtha. 'It was Dinu-babu who had Champak murdered, by Malay.'

'He was a front for Bhabani-babu,' said Abhik.

–And it was Tapan who killed Bharat and Dinu-babu.

–He's also a front for Bhabani-babu.

'Another thing, Abhik,' said Laltu-babu, 'When it comes to a murder, you can call someone guilty only after an arrest, evidence, witnesses. It's best not to talk of these things. The time isn't ripe yet.'

'We'll be careful,' said Tirtha. 'We'll wait and watch. And if criminal activity goes up, we'll intensify our agitation.'

'That's more like it,' said Abhik. 'Nothing like a thrashing from the public.'

'Should I talk to Tapan?' said Somjit.

'No,' Laltu-babu roared.

–This Tapan isn't the old Tapan.

–He has abilities. Which is why Bhabani-babu's recruited him. That the same Bhabani-babu supports us now is something I cannot accept on principle. I have to go, Nandita will be done with her singing lessons. The road through the market is terrible.

'In that case, what are you sitting there grinning for?' said Babul.

–I'll go now, Laltu-da, Tirtha-da.

After he left, Abhik said, 'Let's go with him. It's a bad area, there'll be other girls going home too.'

*

Somjit could hear the roaring from afar. Then he saw the crowd. 'Nandita!' he said and ran.

Tapan had grabbed someone. He was beating him up. His low-pitched, angry tirade could be heard. 'You'll die if I beat you up any more, Rongeen, that's why I'm letting you go.'

Then he announced, 'The old days of catcalling and chasing women and humiliating them on the streets around the station and the bus-stands and the markets are gone. I won't tolerate it while I'm here. Tell the others too. All of you can go now. Don't be afraid. If any of them tries to insult a woman after this, I'll show them what's what.'

The crowd was silent.

–Go on, carry on now. It's your town, you can walk around fearlessly. It had become difficult for women to protect themselves around here, hadn't it? I'll change all that.

Rongeen's mouth and nose were smashed. A police car drew up. A nervous OC inside.

–What's the matter, Tapan-babu?

–The usual. Eve teasing. Not any more. Someone take Rongeen to the hospital.

'How could you beat him up like that?' someone spoke up.

–Barely touched him. I'm Tapan, you think he'd survive a real beating? From now on, it's not just him. Anyone who does it will be punished.

'Should we take him away?' asked the OC.

–Take him.

–And then?

–Shave half his head and let him go. I saw a police super-intendent in North Bengal do it.

Tapan walked away. Somjit's eyes were full of questions. Tapan didn't look at him.

Tiger walked alongside.

–So, you've started right away.

–The sooner the better.

–Somjit and Abhik were dumbfounded.

–It's just begun. We'll continue as long as possible. Must sit with everyone tomorrow, explain the plan. Come, let's go to the police station once.

*

The OC was surprised, fearful.

–You needn't have come yourself.

–Where's Rongeen?

–At the hospital, to have his wounds dressed.

–I might do such things many more times. Our own workers might come to the police station, that is to say, you will pick them up. But no police torture. I repeat, no torture. Do you understand?

–I do.

–There are a few more things you have to understand. Don't pick up innocent people at random and harass them. All cases must go from lock-up to court within twenty-four hours. And the number of lock-up deaths and suicides must come down.

–You astonish me.

–I'm not here for a short time, I'm here to stay. All businesses will continue as usual. Your interests will be looked after. But everyone will have to change the pattern of their work. The public hates the police. You're here to cut down crime, so you will. But do some public service as well. So that the public is happy. Our public is delighted when they see the police stirring even an inch.

–I'll keep that in mind.

–Send Rongeen home when he's back.

–I will. Why don't you leave now.

'You carry on,' Tapan told Tiger, 'I can go on my own.'

–The streets are dark.

–You'll be going alone too. No one will touch me right now, I'm here to stay for some time.

–Be careful.

*

This one act of Tapan's threw the town into severe disarray. 'How could Tapan end up doing what we were meant to do?' said Abhik.

'Tapan's never touched drink,' said Somjit, 'nor misbehaved with women.'

'He's done deeds that are far more horrible, far more condemnable,' said Nandita. 'Still I'll say he saved us today. Besides, he has quite a personality.'

– That's true, he's always had one.

'But I don't trust them,' continued Nandita, 'this is nothing but a stunt.'

'But why?' Abhik asked.

'Let's wait and watch,' said Somjit.

*

Dinu-babu's house was transformed. A sign went up on the outhouse: 'Basundhara: Land and Property Development and Low-Cost Home Construction'. The business had been named after Bhabani-babu's late wife. Mohanlal-babu was the president of the company's board, and Tapan the managing director. 'Manage it, run it too—it's a good plan,' said Malay.

Shuku-babu said, 'Got to admire Bhabani. Not like his wife died just the other day. Oho, like Ma Durga she was. He hasn't forgotten her yet. Could have added a picture of her, though.'

The outhouse was far from small. In his heyday, Dinu-babu would host up to ten people here. Shuku-babu said, 'It's all being furnished, Tapan. Come, choose your room.'

A flight of stairs led from the garden behind the building to the first floor, where there were three rooms, a bathroom and a covered veranda.

'The corner room,' said Tapan. It had an attached bathroom. 'I need net on the windows. There's a bed and a cupboard already. All I need is a desk and a chair.'

–Nothing else?

–What else?

–A Godrej cupboard with a lock, of course. You take the entire floor, your people will stay here too.

–How long will it take?

–A week or so.

Shuku-babu shook his head. 'Dinu used to say he'd give up the big house and move in here. Just his wife and him. But man proposes, god disposes.'

He looked up at Tapan.

–Where there is birth, there is also death. Everyone has a life-span, it's all been measured out. I have just the one daughter. Matched horoscopes to get her married, but in three years she became a widow. Her son, Bibhabasu Dutta, you may have heard of him.

–Footballer.

–Footballer, swimmer, first boy in school. Inheritor of all I have. His father's brothers didn't have sons, he was the jewel in the family crown. Who would have imagined he'd step on a rusty nail, die of tetanus?

Shuku-babu sighed.

–My daughter went almost mad with grief, her mother took to her bed. I don't think about these things any more, I just keep doing my work. Who knows what will happen to all this. I've donated some money to the Jagattaran Matth, they'll give me a room. That's where I'll go in the end.

–What about your brother, Mukut-babu?

–We fell out long ago. I guess his sons will inherit all this. Whatever fate decrees.

His daughter widowed and his grandson dead, why was Shuku-babu still helping Bhabani-babu? For more money? Money for what? Shuku-babu's daughter used to be so lovely-looking. She had even studied for a few years. He spent a fortune marrying her off to a rich man's asthma-afflicted son, a man much older than her. Why had he chosen such a groom?

–I think about it sometimes. She was in love with Dr Mandal, would it have been better for her to have married him? No one in our family has ever had a love marriage. And . . . the horoscopes matched too. Anyway, we can inaugurate the office in a week.

–We're supposed to sell land, but where's the land?

–Bhabani-babu and Mohanlal bought sixty bighas of rice fields in Nabal-Chandighat long ago. I made them buy it. We could tell that this government would come to power. And we also knew that once they did, they wouldn't allow anyone to hold on to excess land.

–The land must be along the railway lines.

–Of course. Nakul Biswas' village, he was hanged during the freedom movement.

–Who owned all that land?

–Who do you suppose? Some belonged to the zamindar, some to the farmers. They wouldn't have been able to hold on to it, so pressure was applied and they agreed to sell.

–And now?

–Develop the land, sell it for building houses.

–Will anyone buy?

–What do you mean will anyone buy? Look at how Kanchrapara and Naihati are expanding, even our own town is growing day by day. Just have to offer the right bait. Excellent prospect. National highway to the east, railway line to the west.

–But there's no way to get there.

–Don't you read the papers? People are putting pressure for a railway station. There will be one soon, just let the Congress come back to power in Delhi.

–They will?

–Of course. Who else but them? Who got India Independence? The Congress, who else.

–Who knows.

–Let these people remain here, and that lot over there. We'll have a Shahid Nakulnagar station there in no time. You were worried about how to get there? Take a train to anywhere you want. Calcutta is just an hour and a half away. No end of buses on the highway. Then there are the lakes, just wait till the government starts fisheries there. The land can be carved up into smaller plots and sold. I'm telling you, Tapan, people will be relieved to move into more open spaces.

–Who will develop the land?

–Basundhara Company. Housing is a huge problem. If you go to Calcutta, you'll see what a big township the government has built between Jadavpur and Tollygunge, it's called Golf Green. The government will buy land around Calcutta now and build more housing complexes. It will happen here too.

–Will you also buy land in the town?

–The state will do its own development on its own land next to the station field. But wherever I find some property . . . there's Kusumpur in the north. Leave all that to me.

–I have no idea about any of this.

–How will you have any idea? Don't get me wrong, people realize the value of land and houses only when they have some of their own. You never had any, so you don't know. Now you'll see, if your fate says so, you'll have a house too. Ever read *Kathamrita*?

–No time to read Ramkrishna yet.

–Everyone can read *Kathamrita*. Try it. Thakur says: Money is dust, dust is money. He was a true seer, anyone who touches the dust of the earth is reaping money now. Anyone who gets into the business earns lakhs. Look at the high-rises coming up in Calcutta, with hundreds of flats being sold. The family of my brother-in-law's brother-in-law, the three Talapatra brothers, they're building housing estates for middle-class Bengalis, cooperatives, just see how big their office is. Don't mistake Bhabani for a fool, there's more money in business than in goondagiri.

Tapan wished he could ask, 'If that's so, why keep the hooch trade and the byarakbaari going?'

–Your job is to stop trouble if there's any.

'Best if I'm never needed,' Tapan thought to himself.

–But who's going to be with you?

–You mean a bodyguard? I'll find someone.

–Get someone you trust. Whoever you appoint will have to be given a post in the company. Mohanlal will explain.

Tapan didn't think Mohanlal would be particularly enthusiastic about working closely with him. He had become very active for a few days after Dinu-babu was killed. Then the alliance with Bhabani-babu was forged. There was probably one with Sudhin-babu too.

When it came to politics, no one could say with certainty what was possible and what was not.

*

–Rongeen is furious.

'He'll cool down. We need to have a discussion with them,' Tapan told Tiger. 'We must find out whether we can get along with each other.'

–Here, or somewhere neutral?

–You want to look for a neutral place already? We aren't at war yet.

–You think they'll come here?

–Why not?

–They're afraid of you.

–It's best here. After dark. No one will be around. You people can kill me if you want to, and leave via the back staircase.

–What rubbish you talk.

–We have to tell them what Bhabani-babu said. He could have told them himself.

–Very well, I'll tell them.

–They better not start doing their thing before the discussion ends.

–Everyone feels you've got the lion's share.

'I don't want anything,' said a voice in Tapan's head. 'I just want another chance. I want to go away on my own terms.'

'I'd have moved away right now if I could have, Tiger,' he said.

–Tired?

–Probably. But I'm not my own master.

–Your being in this line is itself surprising.

–No, it couldn't have been any other way.

There couldn't have been a different outcome for Tapan. He used to find himself burning with rage. His desperate search for a space to survive had brought him here.

–I'll tell them.

–Where will you stay?

–In Bhabani-da's house, where do you suppose?

–Then I'll meet you soon. Set up the meeting quickly, it's important. Is Rongeen still angry?

–Bound to be, even if less than before. Humiliated in public, after all. But you went all the way to the police station to talk about us, you told them to take him home from the hospital, these are big things, boss.

–How can I allow the police to harass our boys?

–That's why we call you 'boss'. Who else but the boss will think of us? Bhabani-da had me released from the police station, and for Malay it was Dinu-babu who . . .

–In Champak's time.

Tiger was silent.

Tapan clenched his fists.

–A friend of yours . . . He was a good man . . . No more Naxals in the township, or else Malay . . . yet Malay was frightened.

–Yes, the police gave him shelter.

Whenever he recalled this one incident, Tapan's guilt over murdering Dinu lifted briefly. Otherwise, thoughts of Bharat and Dinu and Irani weighed him down.

–Let's go. You've got a fine room, though it's low on safety. But you won't be staying alone.

–What about the rest of you?

–Malay, Thanu, Bomba and I, we all stay at Bhabani-da's.

–And Rongeen?

–Still in the No. 3 slum.

–Has he married?

–Lives with someone. She has a daughter. Rongeen will be killed.

–Why?

–This woman's husband is in jail. Remember the clashes on that side of the railway line? The husband killed Kalo.

–You mean the husband is Goju?

–Yes, he's the one. He'll be out soon. Has been appealing continuously, claiming to be sick. The sentence was for seven years, he's served four already, he'll be out any day. You think he'll let Rongeen keep his wife and daughter and house? Rongeen contributes nothing to the household. She came to me to complain, I sent her away. Told her: Work it out with Rongeen. He's a bastard. Occupies someone else's house, gets other girls in there too.

–Who's going to settle all this?

–He'll have to pay with his life. No. 3 is something else. Constant infights. Labourers and Sahu the contractor are right there.

–Let's go now.

'How're you going to live here?' Tiger said as they went down the stairs, 'I'd have died for fear of ghosts.'

–You're frightened of ghosts?

–Very. But Renu-boudi has given me an amulet, I'm safe as long as I wear it.

–No such thing as ghosts, Tiger. Dead men have no power.

–What do you mean? I know it for a fact. On top of that, the daily pujas at Dinu-babu's house have stopped, his wife used to do all that. Bhabani-babu pays a priest to do it now. Takes care of everything. Be careful of Shuku-babu too.

–Even him?

–When it comes to land, he knows the legal system inside out. He's capable of producing a hundred-year-old document at the drop of a hat in support of one of his claims.

–Let's see. It's a war out there.

*

'Might as well buy a motorcycle now,' Tapan reflected as he walked. It would mean more mobility. Then it occurred to him that his days of going home were coming to an end too. It could become quite unbearable to have nowhere to go.

'Shobuj was here,' Tapan's mother said as soon as he arrived.

–Why?

–Something he wanted to talk to you about.

–Tell him not to come here. I'll meet him somewhere else.

–Don't . . . do anything to him.

–To him? To Shobuj? Do what? Don't worry, I promise I won't.

–He had been to Calcutta. Come and eat, I'll tell you what he said.

–You eat too. Has Baba eaten?

–He's home by eight nowadays, eats and goes to bed by nine.

–He's learnt. Even if late in life.

–If only he'd learnt earlier.

–Tell him he'd better stay this way.

–No need any more. Go wash your hands.

This town had running water. It was an old municipality, the water supply had been set up long ago. But that was all that was townlike about this town. Road repairs, garbage disposal and maintaining the street lights—all these things had gradually become non-existent. The water reservoir was close to where Tapan's family lived, it was an old neighbourhood. The first water connections were set up in this part of the town, they still worked. But, Tapan's mother said, even at the hospital they had to fetch water from elsewhere. Though it was rumoured that, soon, the hospital would have its own deep tube-wells.

Tapan washed his hands and face and changed out of his pants into a lungi. His mother gazed at him. So dignified, so refined in appearance. Who'd say he was a murderer?

–Come eat.

–You eat too.

Mother and son had never eaten together. She would cook early in the morning before going to work, and leave the food for them. She'd be paid five rupees every day. She'd take her own lunch. Tapan, Suku, Buku would help themselves. After Buku dropped out of school, he used to wash the dishes and wipe the floor clean after their meal. Their father was bad-tempered in the morning, drunk at night. How can anyone eat the same daal and potato mash every day, he'd scream at their mother.

–Pour some more money down your toddy drain, that's all you can do, and come back home and shout. Soon, there won't even be daal to eat.

–Where's the fish?

–In the market. Do you think the children ever get any fish to eat?

–Why don't they earn and buy it for themselves?

–Aren't you ashamed of yourself?

And the war of words would begin. And yet Tapan's father had passed his matriculation examinations. If he had been clever enough or even sufficiently determined, he would have got a job at a jute factory. Secured employment for his sons too. Many in the town had done just this, the opportunities existed back then.

When Tapan and his siblings were growing up, the town was teeming with people after the Partition. Those who had come over from East Bengal used to give their children a school- and college-education. But earning a living was impossible. The country had no room for an entire generation of youngsters. Had his father been a good man, Tapan might not have turned into a murderer. Still, despite their father, Suku and Buku ended up as ordinary law-abiding citizens. Two plus two didn't always make four.

Tapan's mother served him his food.

–Two rotis? Is that all you eat?

–For a long time now.

–It's not as though you're having milk or fish or eggs regularly. You have to eat properly. You may live a long time yet, you have to stay strong and healthy. How old are you?

–Twenty years older than you, do the arithmetic.

–Not even fifty yet, Ma, just forty-eight.

–Don't worry, I'll eat.

–I won't be eating at home every day. You have to look after the household. Get a servant, get someone to do the shopping. Eat well.

She sighed.

–I'll do all these things, but you take care of yourself.

–Don't worry about me, I'll be fine.

–But . . .

–I know, everyone thinks of you differently because you're my mother. I'll see, if I can make some other arrangement for you. I'll let you know when the time is right. Suku and Buku should keep their eyes open for a suitable house, I'll buy it in your name. Tell them. Whatever is yours will go to them.

–I will. There's something, though . . .

–What?

−Shobuj said Reba and Shyamal are well. He didn't give me their exact location. Only that they're in Kajal's sister Gauri's house right now, she'll find them a place to stay. Sourav and Swati went too. They all met after a long time. Gauri will enrol Reba for training classes of some kind.

−Very good news. I couldn't do anything for Reba, at least Sourav and Swati have. Which is natural, they're human beings. I'm so unfit to be a human I don't even mention Reba's name.

−Even if you don't, you do worry for her.

−What right do I have to mention her or Shyamal's names? What's this, another dish?

−Aloo, with bori. You used to love it.

−I think your family was educated, Ma, that's how it seems hearing you talk.

−They were. But I myself . . . I let them down, and my own life . . . I don't know what to say.

−Did you go to school?

−Till Class Five. I took over the household when my mother died.

−Anyway. I'll talk to Shobuj. He needn't be afraid.

−You're the one I'm afraid for.

−There's nothing to be afraid of just yet.

She was silent again. It was very difficult to live and move around in a town where you were a murderer's mother. 'Don't worry Ma, I'll see if I can settle you somewhere else. You might be able to breathe more freely in a place where I'm not there, where I haven't done any action.'

Tapan's mother gathered up the dishes.

*

Before going to bed that night, Tapan's fingers touched something as he was putting up the mosquito net.

A tiny package wrapped in pink paper. Bael leaves smeared with sindoor, hibiscus-flower petals. The wrapper, and the words printed on it at Ma Tara Press, were all too familiar to Tapan since his childhood. 'Shonkota Kali, slayer of all obstacles, call her name to dispel all fear, dismiss all distress, pray to her with all your devotion on Tuesdays and Saturdays, and she will protect your life, save you from disease and danger and vanquish sixty-four different kinds of trouble and torment for you. Buy the book of the Mother, and read for yourself the incredible tales of those whom she has blessed with her benediction.'

This avatar of Kali was one of the pillars of the town's ancient belief system. All the old residents knew the story of how the idol had been discovered. Even today, at her temple, on the road leading to the crematorium, goats were slaughtered in her name. Many townspeople prayed for her help, promised her many gifts and sacrifices in return. Some years ago, a naughty boy named

Tapan used to pray to this Kali before his annual exams, and then again after he had passed them.

Dinu-babu had been to her temple so often. After Champak was killed, he'd made the goddess an elaborate offering. 'I'd made a promise, I'm fulfilling it now,' he'd said.

Tapan's mother had prayed there, perhaps she had made a promise too. Tapan felt as if someone had punched him hard. She hadn't dared tell him, just left the sacred flowers beneath his pillow. What will the goddess do, Ma? He wanted to hold his mother close, comfort her. But he had never made that entirely natural gesture all his life, how he could he do so now? He couldn't tell even her that flesh-and-blood Bhabani-babu was far more powerful than the stone-and-clay goddess.

Who had been rescued from a crisis by praying to Kali? This was a time of crisis, a grave crisis. Still, Tapan carefully put away the flowers his mother had left for him.

The unceasing anxiety in her eyes, her stricken condition, these flowers—all of these were making Tapan vulnerable. But Tapan couldn't afford to be vulnerable. He would have to leave home as fast as possible.

*

Tapan was sitting in a chair. Malay, Tiger, Rongeen, Thanu and Robi were in chairs too, or on the bed.

'Boss, we need to improve our seating arrangement,' said Tiger. 'How can the boss not have a drawing room?'

–There's one coming up downstairs.

–It's so simple here. Were you brought up in a mission?

–Was I brought up at all?

–Never mind, get to the point.

–What we have to understand is that politics has changed. The old rules no longer apply.

'Will these people change everything?' said Thanu.

–They're not happy with us. There's no reason to be.

–Do we have to keep them happy?

–We have to change the way we do some things. Rongeen is angry about what happened the other day, and well he may be. But I will not tolerate bad behaviour with women. If we can control ourselves on this one matter alone, people will not consider us monsters.

–What else?

–In a minute, Malay. I don't want to interfere in your personal affairs, but collecting rent from shopkeepers or beating up people at the slightest excuse are not things that I will allow.

–Should we become monks, then? Or hermits?

–You will remain who you are. Bhabani-da is the one demanding all this, Tiger knows. At least six of the hooch dens have to be shut down. Two in the Dalit slums, one in the market, one near the hospital. You can choose the other two yourself.

–How will that help?

–People will be happy to see the more visible hooch dens being shut down. Tirtha and the rest of them want the same thing.

–What does that leave us with?

–Get the hooch made, supply it. The market is huge, what's the problem?

–The Dalit slum area . . .

–Those who are addicted will find their way to the booze, no matter where. The main thing is there must be a change in attitude.

–There could still be trouble.

–I'll take care of it. Why should there be any if we behave ourselves?

–Anything else?

–Don't provoke anyone into a gang fight. The police are also telling us to mend our ways. That's all.

'No one told us anything like this in Dinu-babu's time,' said Rongeen.

'But Dinu-babu is gone, Rongeen,' said Tapan softly.

–He used to help you too.

–No. I'm not Dinu-babu's man, never was. Get your facts right.

–I won't call you boss.

–No need to.

–I'll never think of you as . . .

– . . . anything but a murderer. I'm not asking you to. But I'm asking you to remember that murderers do murder.

–Not today, I'll speak up when the time comes.

–By all means. If it's worth listening to, I will.

'Are we done?' said Tiger.

–Absolutely.

–End of meeting, then. Shuku-babu has started a new company. He did a puja. Here, have some prasad, all of you.

'Sandesh only?' said Thanu.

–Boss doesn't drink. Don't worry, I'll pay for the drinks today. Military rum. But this I can say with my hand on my heart, whether it was Bhabani-da or Dinu-da, neither of them ever had a heart to heart chat with any of you like this.

'Never mind,' said Malay. 'I'm thinking it's not safe for Tapan to be staying alone here.'

–We'll make some arrangements, don't worry, Malay.

–When are you shifting?

–Any day now. Might as well.

Tiger handed out glasses of water. They drank, and then left.

Locking the door, Tapan went downstairs. 'I'm leaving,' he told the caretaker.

–Have you locked the back door?

–I have.

*

Tapan walked off towards the market. The Bengali film *Arohi* was being screened again. A glum Shobuj was seated on a bench at a tea shop. One cinema hall probably wasn't enough for such a sprawling town.

–Shobuj.

–Tapan-da.

–Come, I have to talk to you.

Shobuj moved numbly, mechanically.

–Let's go sit in the park.

There was an open expanse beyond the market, caked in dirt, piled high with scraps of paper and garbage. 'A park will come up here,' Nanda-babu had said. It hadn't. Still, everyone called it the park.

–Too dirty.

–Let's sit in a public place. Or you'll be afraid.

–All right.

They sat down in the middle of the open space.

–Wouldn't have been bad if it had been a park.

–Who'll make a park, Tapan-da? You think anyone cares for the town?

–What did you want to tell me?

–I need a job, Tapan-da.

–With me?

–Didn't study, I'm nothing but a loafer. What should I do? Ma gives me hell at home: Look at your brother and look at you. How much do you think I earn from selling movie tickets on the black market?

–Have you tried asking Tirtha? He might be able to put in a word with Sudhin-babu and get you some work somewhere.

–Tirtha-da's politics is the opposite of Dada's . . . he didn't even talk to Dada after Dada got out of jail . . . The Home Guard was hiring . . . wanted character certificates . . . Who's going to give me one, tell me?

–You didn't talk to your brother?

–What can he do? His own situation . . .

–What can you do? You've got a good physique . . .

–You're starting a big company . . .

–How many young men like you, Shobuj?

–Plenty.

–No, I mean those who can be trusted . . .

–There are seven or eight of us, close friends.

–You don't drink, I hope.

–No, no, of course not.

–How do you get by?

–I'm hardly getting by.

–I'll look out, Shobuj. I promise. But if I get you a job, you've got to do it well.

–With you, Tapan-da?

–No, Shobuj, not with me.

–You beat up Rongeen the other day, everyone's stunned.

–You don't spend time with them, I hope.

–No, I'm afraid to.

–I'll look out. Here, take this money.

–A hundred!

–Buy some clothes. And stop this ticket business. It isn't good work.

–Keep an eye out for a job for me.

–I will.

–Sometimes, I feel like doing something drastic.

–I know. I used to feel that way too.

Shobuj had a cleft chin, he was dark but good looking. He barely resembled Shyamal. Tapan knew how Shobuj felt, there was a time when he would be seething too, all the time, which was why Bhabani-babu's bait had worked. Bhabani-babu would hold public meetings now with Sudhin-babu. It was Tapan whom everyone could call a murderer.

–Let's go.

–Most of us wouldn't be antisocials if we had jobs. No one respects us. Ma still calls me a thief because of something I did at home long ago.

–Didn't you have a sister?

–A cousin. Everyone's the same, Tapan-da. Her husband has a big medicine shop in Dum Dum. Knows so many people, those who run nursing homes. Ma requested them to give me a job. I told my cousin, 'Let me clean the shop.' But she said, 'I know you, you'll steal.' Don't talk about them. Dada got into politics, stopped visiting us.

–How do you get by?

–Ma and I live in a single room. Dada too, when he was here. The other two rooms are on rent. Someone's set up a paan shop beneath the mango tree. We barely manage. Or do you think Ma would have to work, ferrying little girls to school?

–Come on, it's getting late. I'll take care of you. But your mother and brother won't object, will they? If you work with me?

–Who do I belong to, Tapan-da? Dada might actually be pleased if I find some work.

–Your sister-in-law might be angry.

–How often do I visit them anyway? If I don't get work, I'll have to become a thief, a petty crook. That was how Preetam was killed, lynched by a mob after he was caught stealing.

–Who's Preetam?

–Lived in No. 3. You know what No. 3 is like, they beat you till you die.

–Don't worry about that. My only concern is, what if you're in danger because you work with me?

Shobuj smiled. His teeth gleamed white.

–I'll be temporary, right? We'll never be permanent, Tapan-da. You could say we're caught in a pincer. Can't be a Preetam, we're from well-bred families, we're gentry. Ma says so, but it's a lie. Baba dressed wounds in the hospital, died before his time. Dada used to coach young students to pay his way through college. He left home, did time in jail, came back. Ma is nothing but a maid at the school. What makes us gentry? Champak-da's parents were gentry. When Champak-da died, they left the town. Tirtha-da loathes us. Somjit-da at least talks to me, he gave me a cigarette once.

–Go into the town. Listen to everything. Report to me.

–I had to report to Bhabani-da. He would scold me if I didn't. But I'll tell you.

–Come on, let's go.

–Everyone's seen me talking to you. They'll think of me differently now.

–Come on. I might take you along when I go out tomorrow.

–Some work?

–Let the company get going. You're on my payroll now. I'll pay you depending on how well you do.

FOUR

No one in the town had imagined that Basundhara Company would flourish so rapidly.

Everyone had been keeping a strict eye on Tapan. Tirtha said, 'Nandita was right, this is a stunt.'

'How can you call it a stunt when people are happy?' Somjit said.

The townspeople were genuinely pleased. Tapan had scoured the town from one end to the other with Shobuj, Kush, Kshiti and Biru, he on his motorcycle, they on their cycles. 'Deduct the cost of the two-wheelers from my earnings,' Tapan had told Bhabani-babu. 'These are investments. We need the town's goodwill, after all.'

– So you're taking Shobuj into your team?

– Who among the older recruits can you depend on besides Tiger? The people who used to misbehave with women—can I have the same people say that the women are safe now? The people who ran the hooch dens—can I use that lot to stop the trade now?

– This will prove useful for you.

–Who am I, Bhabani-da? You're my boss.

–I want *you* to be the boss.

–That's what I'll be. Just that I think it can be done without terrorizing people.

–Try it, you have a free hand.

–You'll see for yourself, even No. 3 will become loyal to you.

–My goodness, you know whose den that is?

–Wait and see.

–But why will you pay for the cycles?

–I'll give them to the boys.

–Gift?

–No, investment. Those who've never got anything, they succumb easily. I can tell from my own example. They're grateful. You picked me up from the streets, I'm grateful still.

–Very intelligent words, Tapan.

–Tirtha and the rest of them will also pipe down. They have some questions about your alliance with Sudhin-babu, your proximity to him. Those will go away.

–I see you understand policy too.

–I've watched you and I've . . .

–Learnt? What?

–Every problem holds its own solution. You have to adjust to the circumstances, or things go wrong. If I have to stay in this line, I have to learn from you.

–Good, you've realized it. Dinu didn't want to learn anything. Wanted to gobble up everything himself.

–Didn't he give you a cut?

–Long story. Never mind, we mustn't speak ill of the dead. So you're not working with Malay and the boys?

–Can't trust them, Dada, and that's the truth.

–Are your boys tough enough?

–Of course. Like I was. They'll learn.

–This isn't a bad thing you're doing. The town will realize you're trying hard to stop the criminals, even if you don't succeed entirely.

–Yes, simple logic.

–Good people are joining the company. People we know.

–I see.

–Like Mihir-babu of Beldanga. Big contractor. Offices in Calcutta, in Keshtonagar. Built health centres not only in Paruldanga but elsewhere too, does highway repairs. Now building massive government quarters in Siliguri. You can't tell by looking at him what his true worth is. Rajat-babu is a cement contractor. Chosen a good line. He's secured a huge quota, making money hand over fist. Arun Singh is a king. Got a steel quota, keeps getting contracts from the Railways. Mohanlal's paternal cousin Sohanlal gets all the projects for railway stations in North Bengal.

–Will they be part of the company?

–Of course. Rajat-babu is from Chakda, Arun is from Belgharia, he's the only one who lives in Calcutta. Sohanlal is based in Kanchrapara.

–Doesn't he have a transport company too?

–A very big one. In Dunlop. They were all Congress people, they're still with the Congress. Extracted all their benefits directly from Delhi. You think I could have done without them? Sudhin-babu—let me tell you something with sincerity, Tapan, mark my words—Sudhin-babu and his people have always been anti-Congress, they will stay that way. They don't have the capacity to realize where the real money is. They're here to do some good work, why not let them do it? I don't know how long they will be in power, but by then we'll have developed the land and exited. Those who have made money already, they won't switch allegiances. The Congress is still a beehive loaded with honey.

–Tiger's very keen on . . .

–I know, a heavy truck. Goods carrier. He needs money, how much can he make from the byarakbaari anyway? He could have done it, Sohanlal would have made sure, but would Tiger listen? I told him: You took out one of his people in Dhanbad. They didn't take action only because you're with me. Of course, you did something for Sohanlal too in Howrah after I introduced you to him. But don't you think you've shot yourself in the foot?

–I didn't know this.

–I told you because you're faithful. You must understand, I can't tell everyone.

–You said the company will work in Chandighat.

–Yes, there's a town coming up, a satellite town. And once the company's established, we'll also work on government housing projects around Calcutta.

–Will you build a house there?

–All of us will. Remember, the price of land never goes down. A small house opposite the lake for myself . . . have to live somewhere in my old age, after all. This house is in your boudi's name. The house in the town I'll sell off.

–Can I say something?

–Of course. Don't hesitate. Rabindranath Tagore has said: He who is bewildered by hesitation insults himself. I know some stuff too, my older brothers are all highly educated after all. I'm the only uneducated one. What do you want to say?

–Nanda-babu didn't build the park he'd promised, beside the market. Why doesn't the company put up railings, clean it, plant some flowering trees, fix a set of taps and donate it to the town? The municipality can maintain it. The company will earn a lot of goodwill.

–Good idea. Not that it will remain a park, given the location. There'll be meetings, plays. Still, I'll tell them, let's see. Do you know what I'm going to do with my house? Can you guess?

–What?

–Nursing home. Dr Mullick's been chasing me. I'll lease it out. Renewable.

–Where will Tiger and the others live?

–Have to think about it. They'll have housing problems too. Didn't I tell you housing was going to be a big problem?

–Will you begin with Nabal-Chandighat?

–I'll launch two projects simultaneously. Four identical four-storeyed buildings on ten bighas of land, on the other side of the station, twelve flats in each. Ananda Talapatra will do the publicity, the plans will reach you. There'll be so much work, you won't have time to breathe.

A nursing home, a new house, how much more financial security did Bhabani-babu need? He was almost sixty. How many houses could Boudi and her daughters occupy?

–I'll take my boys as staff.

–Go ahead. Let them make some money. Four boys. Let them make a couple of thousand in all every month.

Bhabani-babu waved his hand. Meaning, he wasn't interested in wasting time on such trivial matters.

–Your earnings are accounted for too. Shuku and Mohanlal know. Don't worry about it.

–I won't.

What use would worrying have been anyway?

*

When he got back to the town, Tapan went around with Shobuj and his team, telling all the shopkeepers not to allow anyone to take anything for free. Nor should they give money to anyone. He'd also said that if anyone misbehaved with a woman, they should let him know at once. 'Tell me directly, don't be afraid.'

No one in the town had heard such a thing before.

But when the hooch dens in the Dalit slum were shut down, everyone was absolutely astonished. The dens near the market and the station were dismantled too.

'Leave something for us to do,' the OC said.

'You've had plenty of complaints from the town,' said Tapan, 'but you took no action, I don't know why. But I'm telling you now, make sure no new dens come up where we've shut down the old ones. You'll get my cooperation, not opposition.'

The town realized that the old familiar faces were not to be seen any more. Gripped by terror once upon a time, the people understood that Tapan had not given them false assurances.

Malay said, 'No more protection money, then?'

Tapan said, 'If you want it, take it from those with black money, but not yet.'

–And do nothing till then?

–You're coming to work here.

–This isn't my line of work.

–What's your line of work?

–Are you joking?

–I never joke.

–Are you telling me you don't know?

–I'll let you know another day. But Malay, I've told you before and I'm telling you again, Bhabani-babu has agreed to all of this. We can't survive on muscle-power alone.

–Dinu-da never spoke this way.

–How do you expect me to talk like him? People are different.

–You're doing all this to increase your own popularity.

–No, Malay. Look around you. Did you see their meeting at the jute mill the other day? Did you see the crowd? People have voted for them with great hope. Time doesn't stand still, don't forget the demonstration at the college a few days ago because of just one professor's bad behaviour.

–How the town has changed.

–It's changing, yes. You must believe me when I say I have no enmity with any of you.

–How? When it came to Dinu-da . . .

'Dinu-babu didn't induct me, he inducted you. And what did you do?' Now Tapan was shouting. 'You're the one who talked about killing him. You, Malay . . .'

–All right, all right.

*

Tirtha and his associates were talking about Tapan.

–It's not adding up, Tirtha.

–Abhik, this is nothing but fear. He's seen our strength and been afraid.

–Afraid of what? He's not in politics.

Nandita said, 'If the police had done their job, Tapan wouldn't have had this opportunity today. The police could have stopped these things.'

–Why should the police stop anything? They used to get a cut.

–Even from harassing women?

–No. But it was the same goondas, so the police didn't catch them.

Laltu-babu said, 'Fear or deference, how does it matter? This is the time to strengthen our organization.

'Yes,' said Tirtha, 'we should form a citizens' vigilance committee and keep a check on such activities.'

There was laughter in Somjit's eyes. 'And hand them over to the police if we catch them?'

–Yes, then it's up to the police.

–What if they don't do anything?

–We'll protest.

–Tirtha-da, think of an action-oriented plan.

–Tapan's taking help from criminals too.

–One criminal can only take help from another. Mind you, Shobuj used to come to you so often, asking for work.

–Shyamal's brother?

–Shyamal has married Reba and left. Shobuj and he have nothing in common.

Tirtha smiled slightly. 'I can see a pattern,' he said. 'Tapan, Shyamal, Champak, Sourav and Kajal were all classmates. The others went to college, only Tapan became an antisocial. He even became a Congsal.'

'Are we going to forget the truth by using the word *became*?' said Abhik.

–What are you trying to say?

–What about Bhabani-babu's role? It was he who recruited Tapan.

–Tapan is the subject of discussion now. He got out, came to the town. And then Champak was . . . er . . . murdered. I think Tapan and Shyamal had a connection of some sort. Why else would Shyamal marry a murderer's sister, or Tapan give a job to Shyamal's brother?

'Yes, a circle of evil,' said Babul.

'Shyamal and Reba's relationship is an old one,' said Nandita. 'I also know that Shyamal had a condition: that Reba would have to forego her relationship with her brother. She cut all ties with Tapan before she left.'

–How do you know all this?

–Reba used to talk to me. She told me: I hate the sight of my brother. Even his shadow startles me. Ma can visit me if she wants. I never had a relationship with my father, and I never will. I had relationships with my other brothers, those will remain. Just like Shyamal, I have set a condition too: I will not let Shobuj live in my house. I want to lead a clean life.

–So what does it all add up to?

'We'll keep doing our work,' said Somjit. 'Hooch is no longer being sold from the Dalit slum, we can focus our attention there.'

–That's too much, Somjit.

Tirtha's group didn't get around to doing anything for the Dalits. They remained as they were. Twelve years later, another hooch den came up at the same spot, because by then the place had become the realm of criminals.

'Tapan will become popular,' said Abhik.

–They're still selling hooch next to the crematorium.

–That one will stay. The doms like to drink. Plain and simple: Tapan has taken some steps that were necessary. We didn't, he did.

–And he's earned the gratitude of shopkeepers.

–They can't be ignored.

–I'm not ignoring them.

–They voted for us too. They do expect something in return.

'The girls are all saying that no one thought of their safety earlier,' said Nandita.

–That's nothing but Tapan bluffing.

*

Tapan proved soon afterwards that he wasn't bluffing at all. There were many kinds of men who misbehaved with women. The contractor's exploits had ensured that the nurses' quarters in the hospital had collapsed. They hadn't been rebuilt. The nurses were living in the TB ward, which wasn't open to the public yet. It was behind the hospital, at a distance from the main building.

Some people in the town had made quite a bit of money now. Such as Abja-babu, the ration dealer, or Ratan-babu, the permanent dealer for several large pharmaceutical companies. Abja-babu's son Joy, Ratan-babu's nephew Chand and three of their friends used to make the nurses' lives miserable. They moved about on scooters, kept their sideburns, wore dark glasses in the evening and cat-called at the women.

'Joy's gang is chasing a nurse named Sumana,' Biru told Tapan. 'They plan to abduct her, threatened to throw acid on her face if she talks.'

–Who told you?

–My mother cooks for them.

–Acid!

–That's the threat. Before this, there was another nurse named Ruma . . .

–Did they attack her with acid?

–No, they abducted her. Then abandoned her later in the field near the power company's office.

–No one filed a case?

–Who would? Ratan-babu's nephew Chand is one of them. Ratan-babu is very influential.

–What happened to Ruma?

–Quit her job and left.

–Don't the other nurses complain?

–No, Tapan-da, whom can they depend on? Everyone fears for their lives. For their lives, for their honour, for their safety from acid attacks.

–When do the boys go there?

–Just before evening. They gather at Bhanu's stall beside the station. Maybe they take drugs there, I don't know. Then they go to the nurses' quarters.

–In the hospital itself?

–Yes, yes, the hospital is like a second home for Chand.

–All of you stay with me this evening.

*

Biru and the others were carrying cycle chains, Tapan too. It was around seven in the evening. The doors and windows of the nurses' quarters were shut, the lights were on inside.

Neither Chand nor Joy had expected resistance. They had parked their scooters and were about to climb onto the front veranda. Tapan grabbed Joy first, and his companions the others.

–Hey, let go.

–Recognize me?

–What? We . . . I . . .

–Remember I said I'd teach you a lesson if I found you mistreating women here? You don't seem to have realized that Dinu-babu's era has ended.

–I'm . . . Abja-babu's son.

–Let's see whose father saves you now.

They were beaten up with expert skill. A crowd gathered at their screams. Tapan punched them systematically, continuously.

Eventually, he let the bloodied, exhausted young men go: 'Anyone who harasses women in this town will meet the same fate. I know many things go on at the hospital. I don't give a damn whether you're a member of the staff or your father is a hotshot.'

The windows of the nurses' quarters had opened. 'Well?' said Tapan loudly. 'Still want to pick up one of the nurses? Tell me, so I can cut off your head before I go.'

He gave a kick to Joy's head with these words.

–No . . . never again . . .

–Even killing the lot of you won't calm me down. And you—the public—you know what they've been doing, why haven't you beaten them up yet?

'The police doesn't act,' someone shouted.

–Let the police rescue this lot. Come on, let's inform the police station. Let them remain here.

–They'll run away.

–They can't even get up. Well, Chand? Are you going to run away?

Chand groaned.

*

'What you've done this time . . .' the OC said.

–Is too much?

–I mean, Abja-babu, Ratan-babu . . .

–There's only one punishment for harassing women. You never even touched them. I've done the job for you. Pick them up, let them file a case.

They didn't file any cases.

Their fathers were silent. The boys were treated at Dr Mullick's nursing home. Later, the doctor told Tapan, 'Two of them had fractured ankles, Chand and Joy had broken collar-bones and ribs. Lots of other injuries, but their eyes were saved.

–There will be more such cases if this particular crime is repeated. They think they can get away with anything because they have money.

–In confidence, I can tell you I'm very happy. I had to stop my daughter from going to her music lessons because of them.

–People like you consider us lumpen. But the real rotten lumpen always come from your society, and they'll keep coming.

–My son is studying medicine.

–Your son may be different, but this lot is your equal in money and influence. They're not Shobuj or Biru. Not young men from poor families who have never had enough to eat or an education and have turned into criminals.

–Yes . . . you're right.

*

There was a sensation in the town over the incident. Biru said, 'Some of the hospital staff used to harass the women too.'

–And now?

–Now they're all quiet. Ma said the nurses are full of praise for you.

Shobuj said, 'Somjit-da told me: You boys have done good work, Shobuj.'

–Why don't they do it themselves?

–All they do is organize meetings and raise funds. And you know what? Now they're saying: Bring your complaints to the party committee, don't take the law into your own hands.

Tapan was unmoved.

–Let people do it, then. Let the party show us what it can do.

After this, even the police went after the louts on the streets.

'Go after the rich now,' Tapan told Malay. 'Ratan-babu, Abja-babu, there are quite a few of them.'

–What should I tell them?

–Ask for a monthly cut. They can afford it. Don't pressure on the poor. What are you staring at me for? They used to pay Dinu-babu, didn't they?

–What's the money for?

–Why don't you keep it? Give them protection. You're taking it anyway, from what I hear. Why else would Ratan-babu tell you: Is this the protection you offer for the money you're taking?

Malay began to sweat.

–You can do what you like. But protection doesn't mean letting women be molested.

There was no other topic of conversation in the town besides this. Tapan went to Bhanu's shop the next day.

Bhanu jumped to his feet.

–I don't know anything, Tapan, believe me.

–Why do you let them gather here?

–What option did I have? What if they destroyed my shop?

–Do you sell drugs?

–Search the shop. It's only tea.

–Shobuj and the others will start coming here. They'll pay for their tea. The other lot won't show up if my boys are here regularly.

–They'll really pay?

–Of course. You mustn't give anyone anything without payment.

–Look who's there.

–Who? Can't recognize him.

–Your maths teacher.

–Rebati-babu?

–Yes, he's gone a bit senile. Mumbles to himself constantly. His son got a job, but who knows what he fell ill with, they couldn't diagnose it at the hospital, he died. His daughter-in-law got the job, she's moved to Barasat. Ever since . . . he comes for a cup of tea sometimes.

Rebati-babu! A terror in Tapan's adolescence. The old man stopped in front of him and frowned.

–You're . . . Tapan, aren't you?

Tapan bent to touch the ground in front of Rebati-babu's feet.

–I heard you've done something good. Paltu's mother said. She knows what's going on . . . she goes out. Yes . . . you've ousted evil . . . that's good work . . . made me happy to hear it . . . very good.

Tapan sighed.

–I'll go now, sir. I'm off, Bhanu.

–Take care.

This was something new for Tapan. Bhanu and he roamed the streets together as youngsters, got into fights. Then Bhanu began to hawk peanuts, sell lottery tickets, earned money in some way or another. He kept drifting into gangs, but was a coward by nature. At one time they'd spent a lot of time discussing easy businesses they could get into. Now Bhanu supported himself with his tea shop. He was the one who needed protection.

*

It was Tapan's day to go home.

He went once a month, his mother waited for him to visit.

She surprised him today.

–Someone's waiting to see you.

–Who?

–Sumana. The nurse.

–Here?

–She came to me. I told her: Don't wait here, he doesn't like it. She said: I'm not leaving till I see him.

–This isn't right, Ma.

–I told her.

–Get her here.

Tapan's mother went to fetch Sumana. Slim and nondescript. About twenty-five, in good health. Perhaps it was her age that had made those louts . . .

–Why do you want to meet me?

Sumana hesitated. Then she raised her eyes.

–To convey the gratitude of all the nurses and other women staff.

–Nothing to be grateful for. And please, don't come here to meet me.

–I have no choice but to do this job. If you hadn't intervened the other day . . .

–All right. You can let Biru's mother know if you face this problem again. Or Biru or one of the others at the Basundhara office. Not here.

–I'll keep that in mind. Namaskar.

–Namaskar.

Sumana left. Tapan's mother closed the door behind her.

–They don't understand . . . if they start coming here . . . I have plenty of enemies . . . who knows if they'll attack her . . . it's so easy to teach a woman a lesson.

Tapan's mother sighed.

–Enemies, yes, but there are people who praise you too.

–Never mind all that.

–Why do you say that? I pray at the temple on Tuesdays and Saturdays. Your dangers will slowly pass.

–Did you go to Ranaghat?

–Yes, Suku says even that land near the villages costs about five thousand a katha.

–Let him look for some anyway.

–What are you thinking?

–Did you get your eyes checked?

–I'm going this Wednesday. Your father . . . is getting stomach aches . . .

–Do what you have to. Why tell me, Ma?

–Want something to eat?

She would be upset if he declined. Still he said, 'Not today, Ma, I have things to do.'

–Buku came to Ranaghat too.

–I'm glad they visit each other. Take this money, Ma, put it in the bank.

–Will you wear something if I give it to you?

–Don't, Ma. I know why you want to, but I have no faith.

She fell silent.

–Shobuj comes by, right?

–He does.

–He looks after me, Ma. The flowers you send? He puts them beneath my pillow. They cook for me too.

She sighed again.

–Of course they'll look after you. You found work for them . . . but do you look after yourself?

–Ma. You know how long it's been since I left home, since I've been getting into fights.

–I do. I said so many nasty things to you, I regret it all now.

–But what could you have done? Given the state of things here . . . unemployed sons . . . I don't remember the things you said. What I'm saying now is, you know who I am. Don't worry for me, what's the point? I can't return even if I want to, they'll take me out.

–The police?

–Yes, Ma. Living a life of crime leads to death. Giving it up means an even earlier death. That's why I'm trying to find ways to live, can't you see?

–I hope you are.

Tapan knew none of this would come true. Yet it was as if he wanted to convince himself, and his mother too. So he said,

144

'Maybe if I can make a lot of money and then leave this line, go somewhere far away. Maybe I'll live.'

–Then do that. No matter how far away you are, if I know you're alive I'll be all right. At one point, I'd given up hope . . . but ever since you came back, I've been . . .

Tapan's mother had been toughened by the fire of life. So she said, 'You'd better go now, no need to be out late.'

Tapan patted his pocket. The revolver was there. And the switch-knife strapped to his ankle, as always. There was a glut of weapons after the Liberation War in Bangladesh. He would have to arm Shobuj and the other boys, train them in their use. Or did they know already? Tiger would say, 'If only we could get into the border areas. Arms smuggling is big money. Get rich in no time.'

Who knew whether Tapan would get into that business too.

Tapan stood up. 'I've got to make the company work, Ma,' he said, 'Land is where the money is now.'

*

The company was established. So quickly that it felt like a miracle to Tapan.

The scope of their work expanded so much they had to move their office from the outhouse into the main building, the one that used to be Dinu-babu's home. A new coat of paint, some repairs and a pair of new collapsible gates, and the place was transformed.

The outhouse became Ananda Talapatra's office. Tapan made separate living arrangements for himself on the second floor.

From time to time, Ananda Talapatra came over from Calcutta. The advertisements had to be prepared in the city. Basundhara's Calcutta office, the city booking office, had been set up at Talapatra's residential address.

The full-page advertisements for Basundhara's proposed housing project on the other side of the station, and for the proposed township in Nakulnagar, were dazzling.

Bhabani-babu had indeed said that people would be desperate for a place to live in, but Tapan hadn't realized how right he had been.

Among those who booked the hundred and ninety-two flats at ten thousand rupees each in the housing complex on the other side of the station were people from places like Jagaddal, Naihati and Kanchrapara. But that there were so many in this town itself who were ready to pay so much for flats—Tapan had had no idea. He couldn't even recognize some of the names.

'How will it help you to know who they are?' said Shuku-babu. 'Rajat-babu and the rest of them have all booked a couple of flats too, all under false names.'

–But they won't live here.

–They're not buying them to live in. They'll hold on to them for a while and then sell them.

–Will people buy at one lakh twenty, one lakh thirty?

–You bet they will.

–Will they have to pay the full amount before taking possession?

–No, they'll get some concessions. It's not a government project, after all. There you can pay forty per cent and get possession. Here, you need to pay sixty.

–Will that be enough to build the flats?

–It'll cost us much less than that. We can build a few shops on the ground floor too.

–What about water?

–Everything will be organized, everything. Experienced people are involved. Bhabani-babu has asked for you to be given an option.

–Me? Buy a flat?

–Why not? You don't have to live there, you can sell it later. No problem.

'There's no crematorium nearby. May those who move in have long lives,' said Ananda Talapatra with a smile.

–You'll show people around, Tapan. And once the construction begins, you'll practically have to live there.

–Yes, there'll be material worth lakhs at the site.

'No,' said Mohanlal-babu vehemently. 'Tapan won't live there, he's needed here. You don't know what you're saying, Shuku. Do you think you understand everything? Just take care of the legal side. Tapan will collect the cheques and deposit them, he's needed here.'

–What about the squatters?

–Tapan will evict them.

–And supervision?

–Let Tapan decide who he'll hire. Tapan, you do realize that for some years you'll be able to employ quite a few boys. And remember, you have that flat option too.

–What about my percentage?

–Two thousand a month, for you that is. And if you get, say, another two thousand per flat, that's quite a total.

Tapan realized from their calculations that there would be a minimum profit of twenty thousand per flat.

–At least a hundred flats have been booked already.

–That's true.

–So I'm owed some money.

–Already?

–What does it work out to in percentage terms?

–Do you need money?

–I will soon. I'll take it when I do.

–Look, the work can't start till the squatters are evicted.

–I'll take care of it.

*

'It's a five-lakh game, boss,' said Tiger.

–I was out of focus for a while.

–Will you buy us some booze?

–How can I when I don't drink myself? But if you can't be in the mood without a drink, I'll send Kush to get some.

–No, just give me the money. I don't want to drink with them. There's a new girl, she's very good. I'm keeping her as exclusive. Has a family. Sister's husband sold her, can you imagine? She's landed up here by accident, or else she's a marriage-worthy girl.

–Why don't you marry her then?

–Not possible, boss. Her sister's husband didn't spare her. Ruined her quite a bit. Can't marry her. And as I said, no settlement for me even if I want it.

–You have a yearning for family life. You're young still, you could give up all this.

–I'll be killed. Anyway, you're asking me to leave but you're bringing in new boys. Aren't you putting their lives at risk?

–That's true too. Anyway, you were saying . . . ?

–Remember Sahu? From No. 3?

–He's gone, hasn't he?

–His son Pujon has taken over. He's put people on that land, at least fifty shanties. Runs a hooch den, roaring business. This lot won't be able to evict him.

–He won't go if he's paid off?

–They offered a lakh. He smelt an opportunity and asked for five.

–Really?

–Why not? Do you know who the land belongs to? The haji shaheb, no less. Mohan-babu and Bhabani-da took it on a joint lease. The owners had all gone off to Bangladesh. Shuku-babu produced a false grandson as his heir and made a new lease. Fully legal deed, ninety-nine-year lease.

–All of Mother Earth for free?

–Shuku-babu's done quite a few such deals already. And now the price of land is sky-high. Pujon's trying to make a killing while he can. The area beyond the station is municipal land, everyone knows a thermal power plant will be set up there. That's why they need you.

A vein began to throb in Tapan's forehead.

–I won't tolerate this. They don't know who they're dealing with. Neither money nor my life means anything to me. The day I used my knife for the first time, I knew my life was in peril forever. I'll see this to the end.

–What's the matter?

–It's a matter of respect, Tiger.

In a low but ferocious voice Tapan continued: 'Respect for the murderer. You've brought me in because I'm a murderer, then give me the respect that comes with it. Do other people have to tell me what I'm supposed to do?'

–I should be going now.

–I have to meet Bhabani-da tomorrow. Bring the car keys.

–Who knows if he's there or not . . .

–Don't be afraid. He's made a fool of me, I'll make one of him. But I won't make a widow of Renu-boudi.

Tiger left.

*

Bhabani-babu was startled.

–Frightened? So you know what fear is?

–Calm down, sit down, and then talk.

–Tapan won't be calm, Bhabani-babu. Tapan is a murderer. He who uses a knife knows he will face one too. You got me into your plan to steal lakhs and lakhs worth of money. Even though you knew I was a murderer. What you really wanted me to do was to get rid of Pujon Sahu. You should have told me clearly. I'm offended.

–Not stealing—it's a business.

–Turning black money from cement, iron rods and railway contracts into white isn't business. Profits of twenty, twenty-five thousand on each flat. All of it going into the new township.

–What do you want?

–Every time a flat is booked, as soon as the money is paid, I want my cash at once. Pujon will be taken care of, but it will cost you twice what you paid for Dinu-babu. And I'm going to use this car from now on.

–Good, I see you're ready. You've learnt to bargain.

–Don't provoke a murderer. Anyone who has killed once knows he's no longer responsible for his own life. He becomes reckless, Bhabani-da.

–All right. But not this car, I'll give you a jeep, you need mobility.

–And remember this too: Sudhin-babu's party will create trouble. They're opposed to evicting slums and shanties.

–There'll be no opposition. I contribute to the party fund. You think *they* won't be evicting squatters when the land development begins in a few years? Will the new town in Salt Lake come up by itself, just like that? Evict one lot of people to build housing for another lot. They'll be ready for these things too, in a few years. Until then, we've got to do what we can.

–Won't Tirtha and his group or Laltu-babu's union stop us?

–Laltu-babu is not a fool. You've gained tremendous good-will by putting an end to evil practices. Laltu-babu himself said he'd be so relieved if No. 3 was cleaned up.

–Shan't we offer any money to Pujon?

–We started with ten thousand and went up to a lakh. He raised his price to five. Do you know how much the land cost?

–How much?

–Including registration and formalities, sixty thousand back in the day.

–Who sold it?

–The owner's grandson.

–I have different information. Amiruddin the false grandson got five thousand and skipped over the border. He's in North Bengal now. Anyway, that's none of my business.

Bhabani-babu was silent.

–I'm off now.

–Make sure it's done.

–It will be. But only after I talk to him first . . .

–Whatever you want. I'm the one who insisted on getting you. Mohan wasn't very . . . er . . . keen. I said: He's from this town, must have a soft spot for it because his mother and sister are still here.

–Is that a threat? Why are you bringing my mother and sister into it? I have no relationship with my family. I send money to my mother, that's all. Don't threaten me.

–No, in fact I'm afraid of you.

–No need, you still need me. But if you need someone, you have to deal fairly with them. You haven't done that with me, have you?

–Everyone makes mistakes.

–Yes, Bhabani-da, but it's humans who err.

–What am I, inhuman?

–No, I'm inhuman. You're Superman.

FIVE

'Gangster killed in gang war over old dispute. Pujon Sahu's murderer missing. In the past ten years, the victim . . .'

The news shook the town.

Tapan had counted out the cash. And then gone to meet Pujon Sahu.

Babla trees and clumps of kaash dotted the plot of land on which the proposed Basundhara Housing Complex was to be constructed. Shanties everywhere, with Pujon's house in the middle, the only brick house.

Tapan was there to effect an agreement. It would have been foolhardy to go alone, so he had taken along Tiger and Malay.

–If you're here to cut a deal, why have you brought them?

–Deals need witnesses.

–I don't.

–You're in your own den.

–And comfortably so. What do you want?

–Give up this space, Pujon-babu.

–To Bhabani and Mohanlal? Why? It's lawaris land.

–It's theirs now. Besides, it's for a housing complex. Many people will live here. Everything will change.

–Will I become homeless?

–Take the money.

–How high is the offer now?

–A lakh.

–No.

Tapan said, 'I'm telling you, take the money, go away. And I'll make sure you get a flat.'

–I have the house my father built back in No. 3, what will I do with a flat?

–Think about it.

–Tell them to raise the offer.

–How much?

–I'd said five, I can go a bit lower.

–How low?

–Four and a half.

–Where should I bring the money?

–Will they give four and a half?

–They will.

–Bring it to No. 3.

–You won't go any lower?

–No.

–Then come to the field in No. 3 the day after tomorrow, around eight, say. Pujon's not asking for much, Tiger.

–No, hardly anything.

–Not right for the housing to be held up either.

'Not at all,' said Malay.

–They're working for money too.

–Of course.

–What's that commotion outside?

–They come, they drink, raise a ruckus, do some hanky-panky too. With the girls . . . Can't blame them, everyone needs some comforting.

–Of course, they do.

–You don't drink?

–No, I help others drink.

The transistor was playing. Continuously. Tiger turned the knob. The song grew louder.

–Nice thing you've got there.

–Yes, it's a Philips. Ceylon, Kathmandu, gets all the stations.

Pujon turned the knob to show Tapan how it worked. Tapan leant forward, raised his arm. The knife flew. Lodged itself in the ribs, on the left.

Pujon's mouth opened in astonishment.

This time in the throat, a quick slash to the left.

Wiping the blade on Pujon's clothes, Tapan stood up.

–Let's go. Shut the door. Let him listen to the radio.

Then the jeep. They leave.

Malay said, 'Oh, I'm still shaking. Who takes such risks?'

–No risk, no gain, Malay.

–What if they'd turned up?

–We had guns.

*

Pujon often spent the night in his house on the land, didn't always go back to No. 3. As a result, there was not that much anxiety or panic in No. 3. In that house too, Pujon mostly listened to the radio, stayed in his room. So nobody worried too much about him. His bodyguards had gone off to drink, as they frequently did. They knocked on his door around midnight, then entered.

Then they began screaming.

–There'd be money talk, private, he'd told us to leave. What do we do now?

–Who came to meet him?

–Tapan-babu.

–We have to go to the police.

–Who'll go? And what's the use anyway? The police and Tapan-babu are like flies and honey.

–Still, they have to be told.

–Whoever goes to tell them will be arrested himself.

Alarmed, confused, the men exchanged glances, unsure of what to do.

–Should we get the hell out?

–Why?

–Pujon-babu's dead, who will protect us?

–Ask the old woman.

The old woman—Moti, owner of a hooch den. Dressed in black, she had henna-coloured hair, light eyes and a tattoo on her forehead.

She hauled her large frame up with the help of her stick.

–Pujon-babu's died?

–Yes, Dida.

–No one will protect us now.

–Who killed him?

–If only Pujon-babu had agreed to the money.

–What should we do?

–Go to the police. But take no names.

–They'll evict us anyway.

–We'll tell Laltu-babu. The new government won't evict the poor. We've been here ten years, don't we have some rights?

Pujon-babu said: If you've been somewhere twelve years, you have the right to claim.

*

Everyone at No. 3 gathered around Pujon Sahu's body. The lanes and by-lanes were dreadfully still. Pujon's brother-in-law and nephew waited in the car. Inside the house, his wife and other women were weeping.

Laltu-babu gave no credence to the old Moti and her deputation.

–What possession? Who has possession? If there's possession, there must be documents. Bring the documents, then we'll see. You think living somewhere gives you ownership? By that logic, those who live on railway platforms will say they own the station.

'Oy Laltu,' said Moti, 'then where will we go?'

–Don't ask me, Mashi, I know nothing. Did I ask you to live there?

–No, Pujon-babu did.

–I didn't try to evict you either. Whatever you have to say, go say it to the landowners.

–But we hear your party won't allow slums and shanties to be removed?

–Mashi, demolishing the shanties of hard-working folk, that's one thing. What good work are you doing there that the public will support you? I'm giving you good advice, vacate the place. Or who knows who might beat and break up everything, throw out everyone—what will you do then?

–Go, go, but where will we go?

–I don't know. Have you forgotten, all those days ago, how Tapan thrashed and threw out the old hawkers at the station market?

–You're a rich man, so is Mohan, you will look after each other. The poor have no one.

*

'Why not get the police to beat them up and throw them out?' Mohanlal spoke finally.

'No, why would you beat them up?' said Tapan. 'You should be creating goodwill.'

–What then?

–Give them two hundred per shanty to leave the place. And you'll need a lot of labour. Why don't you use some of this lot for that too?

–Are these . . .

–My conditions, yes. They will end up relocating near No. 3. When you start building there, they'll start to steal your materials, harass you daily.

–I have boys to take care of that.

–You have no boys, not one. It's easy to sit in your chair and talk, go to No. 3 once—why don't you? People are inflamed.

–Ananda said the man was an antisocial.

–Haven't you seen antisocials in Calcutta? That Kamal Ghosh who bought a flat at our project, what great social worker is he? You and your lot need the antisocials. Or what else am I doing here? Don't talk rubbish.

*

The police weren't particularly pleased about Pujon's murder, but the town had a strong response.

'I've worked out Tapan's pattern,' Somjit said.

'Where do you see a pattern?' said an angry, anxious Tirtha.

–Take out the criminals like Pujon and his kind. Because other kinds are stepping up on stage.

–Such as?

–Check who's grabbed the land, who's building the houses.

–Not true.

–Why not? Because Bhabani-babu contributes to the party fund?

–Your words . . .

–I'm here to do politics, I'll keep doing it. But many things don't have my moral support.

–Our meetings are the best place to talk about all this.

–How is it that they got evicted and we didn't say a word?

'What do you mean?' Nandita said. 'They ran hooch dens, gambling dens. If they're not evicted, then who? Be a little realistic, Somjit.'

'I agree with Somjit,' said Abhik. 'Small sins are being uprooted, big sins are taking root. Champak and his group had spoken up against these people. They were afraid of Champak. But they aren't afraid of us.'

–Upper echelons everywhere are merging, why should they be afraid? Only we can bring these issues up.

–Let's see in the coming elections. Just a year or so.

–Have you seen the way they're playing with money? They'll speculate and send the land price soaring, send everything out of the reach of the middle class.

–Will Tapan still be there?

–One Tapan will go, another will come.

No one had imagined that day how much the picture would change in a few years. Criminals would no longer go to Bhabani-babu for shelter, they would find sanctuary with far more power-ful people. Tirtha, Abhik, Somjit, Babul, Nandita and all of them would move away. They would be known as dissidents. Politics and terror would become one in the lower levels of society. Once upon a time, the terror unleashed by the Dinu-babus of the

Congress had made ordinary people helpless and resentful. In those days, this group had stood shoulder to shoulder with the common people and helped them fight back. All these factors led to the creation of the new government. But no one had imagined that one day Sudhin-babu's nephew Aalok would be the new boss in the town. That a large part of a whole new generation would turn into criminals. That corruption would be all-pervasive, that Sudhin-babu and Laltu-babu would amass so much wealth.

No one could have seen the future.

*

The town was quite pleased at Pujon's death. After all, a criminal had been removed.

Alongside the terrorist label, another opinion arose about Tapan: The man's got guts, I tell you. Killed Pujon in Pujon's own den!

Several rumours sprang up at this time.

Tapan had some sort of an extra-powerful amulet.

His guru's instructions, so he never drank, was very respectful towards women.

He could shoot with one hand and knife with the other at the same time.

'So many stories flying around,' said Shobuj.

–Let them fly. Many stories flew about Dinu-babu too. Don't pay attention.

–Why didn't you take us along that day?

The force of Tapan's slap flung Shobuj to the floor. 'No,' Tapan roared, 'I will never take any of you with me. Do you want to turn into me?'

Shobuj rose to his feet.

–Maybe you will, maybe you won't have a choice. But I'm not going to be the one to teach you how to kill.

With a faint smile he added, 'It's not easy to get to the top of this line, Shobuj. Very tough.'

–Very?

–Very. Taking a life in cold blood isn't all that easy.

But it is easy when the blood is boiling.

*

Rongeen had forgotten this. He was inching towards disaster.

Biru brought a young woman to Tapan one day.

–She wants to say something to you.

–Who's she?

–Rongeen-da's . . . you know . . .

A married woman, about twenty-five. With her was a young girl, aged six or seven.

–What do you mean 'you know'? He took me to the Kali temple and married me, put sindoor.

She was weather-beaten but strong and firm bodied, dressed in a bright, colourful sari, gold-plated bangles around her wrists. Necklace and earrings. Silver anklets too. She could have been called pretty had it not been for her acne scars. Her eyes were frantic with fear.

–What's your name, please?

–No need to say please.

–Tell me your name.

–Papia, surname Das, it used to be Singh.

–What do you want to tell me?

–Save me. Have pity on me, save my daughter.

–Biru! Take the girl outside. Now, tell me.

–I'm in great trouble.

–What exactly has happened?

–The girl's father is coming home. Once he's back, he'll kill her, kill me too.

–When is Goju Singh being released?

–There's no justice. He was caught for murder, sentenced to seven years' jail. Kept pretending to be ill, kept making his lawyers appeal. Now his time's been reduced or something—he's coming.

–How did you find out?

–The lawyer is in Naihati. Someone brought me the news. If he comes, he'll kill me. And . . .

–And what?

–This one won't go either. I keep telling him: He's on his way here, leave me. He won't listen.

–Didn't you say you got married to Rongeen?

–Yes, at the temple.

–Well, then?

–He's also taken to torture me. See, I have two rooms of my own. Sahu-babu'd given them to my mother. Not Pujon Sahu, his father.

–Why did he?

–He looked after my mother a lot. It's because of these rooms that Singh married me. He's from Chhapra, owned land and property there, so why marry me? He sold his own land, added a room to the house here, got a water line.

–Do you want Rongeen to leave?

–Let him leave if he has to. Why should I?

–Why did you go off with him?

–I know it was a mistake. I hadn't imagined he'd start a hooch den at home, bring in other women, and not pay a penny to help run the house.

–And Goju will kill you when he's back?

–Surely. He'll cut me up, won't spare the girl either.

–Can't you sell everything and go away?

–Go where? And selling takes time. We'd be saved if this man just left me.

Papia was a veteran of many battles, but the look in her eyes was different now. She needed assurance. But the truth was entirely different. Papia was not Sumana at all.

Frowning, Tapan chose to tell the truth.

–Look, Rongeen alone can't be blamed for everything that has happened, everything that you fear will happen. You're responsible too. One went to jail, you married another. Now this one doesn't want to leave, but Goju Singh's arrival spells danger for you. It was wrong to have involved Rongeen in the first place.

–My mother did it too. My father was put inside for robbing a train in Malbazar. My mother came here and got married again. He gave her nothing either. She got the house eventually because of Sahu-babu's kindness. But she wasn't murdered, she died in hospital.

–I don't know if he'll listen, but I'll talk to Rongeen.

–If you talk to him, he'll run for his life.

Papia left with her daughter.

–Biru.

–Yes, Dada?

–Why do you let such people in?

–Who's going to stop her? She's been coming and going for days now. She's a terrible woman. And what a foul tongue. That mother of hers she was talking about? Not like she cared for her. I hear things. Don't know for sure.

–I don't want to be involved in these dirty things.

–Why should you be? Talking to Rongeen is nothing but a waste of time. He will never give up such a comfortable arrangement. He'll do the opposite of what you say. Let Goju teach him a lesson. And Papia? She always knew Goju would come back. Why didn't she think of this before? No one can do anything about No. 3.

–Nothing's changed.

–Nothing ever will.

*

'Why will it?' said Ananda Talapatra and smiled gently at D. P. Sein, the architect-designer of the proposed satellite township to the west of Nakul Biswas Station. Sein's grandfather used to pronounce Sen as Syan, hilsa as ilsa, used 'mekur' from his East Bengal dialect to refer to their cats. His son began to spell their name as S-E-I-N. So this family was now the Sein family. If some-one asks him, 'Are you Bengali?', D. P. smiles and says, 'We're Indian.'

What else could he say, when his wife hailed from Hyderabad, his elder son-in-law a Maharashtrian from Pune, his younger son-in-law a Jat from Haryana, and his only daughter-in-law a Manipuri, and considering that the languages spoken at home were English and Hindi?

'Think big,' D. P. Sein said. 'You've got so much land here, try out a different kind of model colony. It's close to Calcutta, let it include a supermarket, an amusement park, a hospital, everything.'

–No, the promoters are targeting middle- and upper-middle-class Bengalis. Are you interested?

–No, I prefer Bombay. I bought a flat there a long time ago. There's no point giving new ideas in West Bengal. Other states are creating much better housing complexes.

–I'm wholeheartedly Bengali, though.

–I don't understand how. If only you could see the future, you'd know that Calcutta has none. You think one Salt Lake or one Golf Green can save the city?

–Cities don't die.

–Look at the history of the world, so many cities have died.

–Ancient Rome is gone, but hasn't a new Rome come up?

–Never mind the West, forget India too, look at West Bengal alone, West Bengal. Once it was Gaur, now it's Malda, a small town at best. Calcutta will be choked to death. The population will swell, space will shrink.

−Yet someone like you has booked two flats in Basundhara colony.

−I have two aunts without whose help . . . Both of them were schoolteachers, didn't marry, they're getting on in years. My grandfather gave nothing to my father because he married a brahman girl. Bequeathed everything to his daughters, these two aunts. And they sold the house in Dhaka, everything, to help me. They're the ones who'd like to settle here.

−That explains it.

As they went past the station, went past No. 3, D. P. Sein said, 'This place will stay the same.'

−Why will it?

−What change do you expect?

−It will develop.

−Develop from what?

−It's a den of crime now. Won't stay that way.

−I know that.

−What do you know? You know No. 3?

−Oh yes. Hooch, prostitution, murder, shelter for criminals . . . even the police are afraid to enter.

−How do you know all this?

D. P. Sein had patches of leukoderma around his fingers, at the corners of his lips and around his eyes. Spreading his fingers wide, he looked down at them, and said, 'A friend of mine is a crime analyst. He was researching some areas around Calcutta. Places like these always have a tie-up with crime.'

–Really?

–Don't they? Who's Bhabani-babu? Why all these murders in the town over the past two years? Even now, the man who's working for you . . .

–Softly, softly.

–It's been discussed. These places will stay the same. As stifling as they are now.

–Stay the same?

–It's possible that the population pressure will rise to such an extent and the prospect of real estate become so tempting that someone much more powerful than you will come along and buy up all this, bulldoze everything and throw everyone out.

–Really? When?

D. P. Sein laughed.

–Not anytime soon. Don't forget, there's a different government in power. It isn't possible to displace a couple of thousand people now. The numbers of the poor and lower middle class are still huge in West Bengal. It will be possible once black money circulates freely, when many people make easy money.

–Don't say such things to anyone else.

–Of course not. I like your flats in Calcutta. Extremely economical planning—good. Are you aware of who's buying the flats?

–This is all part of business.

–It'll be safe to live in that housing complex, won't it?

–Oh yes, we can guarantee that. But you mustn't breathe a word about the murders.

–And why should I? I won't be in any danger, I'm your customer, after all.

–Not you, your aunts.

–Oh yes, I can't possibly live in West Bengal, I'll live in Bombay. I'd built a house in Hyderabad, I'll sell it.

Ananda Talapatra gazed at him with great respect.

–You put up in Lansdowne Court when you're in Calcutta, don't you?

–I'll sell that flat too. My aunts live there now, once they move out, I'll sell it.

–Will they live in separate flats?

–They'll live in one, put the other on rent. I think the colony will be a good one.

–Just two women by themselves?

–Yes, that's how they live now. What's this, there are still squatters on the land? I see shanties.

–No, no, most have gone. The rest will go too.

–Who's that young man? Who's he talking to? Striking personality.

–I'll tell you later. Tapan-babu, namaskar.

–Namaskar.

–This is D. P. Sein.

–The one who's buying D3 and D4?

–Yes. This is Tapan-babu.

–Namaskar. Are the squatters still here?

–They're leaving today.

*

'So you're leaving today,' Tapan told Moti.

–Yes, we will. They won't evict us from the railway land too, will they?

–Never seen such a thing happen.

–If they do, will you settle us somewhere else?

–We'll see.

*

'Are you taking a flat too?' D. P. asked Tapan.

–Haven't thought about it yet. I have to go now.

Tapan got into his jeep, Shobuj drove off. Ananda wiped the sweat off his forehead. 'This place used to be a crime den,' he said in a low voice.

–I heard. Once a gang leader died . . .

–Not so loud. You saw the fellow who went off? That's the boss now.

–He, a don?

–No, the boss.

–Same thing. A criminal, right?

–Yes. Let's go back.

–Read history, the history of crime. Criminals kill one another, get wiped out. It has happened so many times. Are crimes any less in Bombay?

–Let's leave, best not to talk about these things here.

–Let me look around before I go . . . I'm paying the entire amount upfront after all. My wife and I plan to travel through Europe and America for a year. All three children are abroad, I won't be back for a while. Let me take a good look at the place so I can tell my aunts all about it. Does the road run past No. 3?

–No, you see the trail on the north? The municipality will tarmac it. Where we're standing now, there'll be a bus stop. And the minute you go to the west, you'll get the highway.

–What a lovely krishnachura! You'll keep it, I hope.

–Can't keep this one. But I'll tell them to plant some trees.

–When does the construction start?

–The MLA will inaugurate it. As soon as he's available . . .

–Politicians, antisocials, black money—this nexus thrives everywhere now.

–It didn't use to be like this here . . .

–You're too young to know. It was very much here. It still is, and always will be. Who's the most famous person in the town, tell me? Anyway, let's get back while there's time. I can tell my aunts I've seen the location. Actually . . . my grandfather joined the education service later. He used to teach in a school in Naihati or Barasat or somewhere. So, my aunts used to visit this area when they were children. They still have a small-town mentality. Oh, isn't that a beautiful sunset?

–Let's go. We have to go past No. 3, after all. So peaceful.

*

The tranquillity that had enchanted D. P. Sein, that same tranquillity was shattered into pieces a little after eight o'clock that night.

The skies above No. 3 shook with repeated explosions, screams and gunfire. The stationmaster informed the OC. Trouble across the railway line, how long before it spread this way?

Abhik and the others went from the club to Laltu-babu.

–Call up the police station.

–I don't even know what's going on.

–What's going on is what always goes on. How many times have we asked for a police outpost there? How much longer will you nurture that No. 3, not even a quarter of a mile from the station?

–You cannot say just anything you want, Abhik!

–You're a leader here. What do you suppose the people think of us? That we're ineffective, useless.

–I'll make a call.

–Why are people going to Tapan to get things sorted? Why should they be under the impression that we're impotent? All of you are making a mistake, Laltu-da. We may lose our acceptance among people one day.

–Will you let me make the call? There's only one exchange . . . if this is how public-utility services are going to function . . . telephone, electricity . . . Yes, yes, give me 912. Keep trying, this is Laltu Bose . . . Yes, 912? Is that the police station? The OC please . . . What's going on? Can't you hear? Or don't you want to hear? What? The driver has gone to the bathroom? . . . Go there at once. But be cautious. That other time the police shot a vendor at No. 3—No, before your time. Go, go have a look.

'It's a hero's return,' Somjit said casually, 'this was bound to happen.'

–Meaning?

–Goju Singh, Papia's first husband, he's coming back home. And letting everyone know that he is.

–What do you mean first husband?

177

–Pukka marriage. With Shonkota Kali herself as the registrar. Divinity after all, one glance and the marriage is sealed.

'Stop talking rubbish, Somjit,' said Abhik.

–The picture's a bit complicated. Because Papia's second husband Rongeen is still with her.

–Second husband?

–Pukka marriage. Shonkota Kali again.

–Are they fighting?

–Goju is on his way with his gang to take control. Rongeen is fighting to keep control. He has a gang too. This isn't oppression of the weak by the strong, nor does it have a political explanation.

–How are you getting all this information?

–Public relations. Not from Tapan.

'If your public relations are so good, then why are the street collections so poor?' Laltu-babu snarled. 'How are we going to manage without contributions from our supporters?'

–I can't put pressure on them. And how will it look if I collect protection money from the poor when it was an antisocial who stopped it in the first place?

–You don't understand.

–Yes, I admit that I don't. I'm waiting for someone to explain it, but no one is willing. I'm not capable of anything besides cultural work.

–Anyway, don't take the shortcut through No. 3.

–Don't forget I'm a product of this town, Nandita. I'm going to the police station.

–I'll go with you.

–No need to come with me at this hour. Let Abhik take you home.

–Be careful.

*

Tapan was at the police station.

'Don't rush me, don't rush me,' the OC had told him. 'Let them use up the bombs, let it quieten down a bit.'

–You think that'll happen?

–What if a policeman dies?

–True, they usually do the killing. But here they could end up being killed. But if the police are on their way, that news is enough to put a halt to things.

–What did Abhik-babu want to say?

–The same old thing. We need a permanent solution to No. 3.

'Won't happen,' said Tapan.

Abhik had spoken to the OC, but it was Tapan who answered. Now Abhik spoke to Tapan directly: 'Does anyone have a problem with a solution?'

Abhik was asking Tapan, but Tapan aimed his answer at the OC: 'There won't be a solution as long as Goju and Rongeen are there. Why don't you take your jeep and go, when do you plan to go?'

Abhik looked at Tapan silently.

–Yes, go quickly. Can't you see how long they've been sitting here for you?

'They who?' said Abhik.

–Beggars, the monkey-dance man. They live by the railway lines too.

The OC made a mental note of the fact that Abhik and Tapan were having a conversation via him. Abhik and Tapan? It didn't add up, but why? He spoke, looking at Tapan: 'Yes, I'll go now. We have just the one jeep, the driver has chronic dysentery, how large is the force here anyway?'

The OC left.

'Go now,' said Tapan. 'They're about to arrive at a solution over there.'

Abhik knew he was doing something he shouldn't. Yet he asked: 'What solution?'

'Either this one will kill that one, or vice versa,' said Tapan dispassionately. 'It won't stop otherwise.'

–What will make it stop?

–Till someone else comes up.

–We need a police outpost there.

–Tell Sudhin-babu, tell Laltu-babu.

Tapan left. He had spoken quite roughly to Abhik. They were on one side, he on the other. They were different. It wasn't as though they didn't know each other. But talk was impossible now. Why was Abhik being so foolish, why was he talking to Tapan?

Tiger was in the jeep. 'Did some plain speaking,' said Tapan. 'The police had better not catch the ones who've run away here. I kept telling him to rush there, he just wouldn't move.'

–What's the point in rushing, Dada? One of the two has to be wiped out before there can be peace.

The people waiting in the portico of the office building seemed to have realized they wouldn't be going home tonight. They had bought bread to eat, and were taking turns to drink water at the tap.

'Should I get rid of them?' said Kush.

–No need, they'll leave on their own in the morning.

The monkey-dance man, the monkey, the beggars and some others had gathered there. Spotting a young girl eating bread, Tapan said, 'Aren't you Papia's daughter?'

She didn't answer.

The monkey-dance man said, 'Her mother left her here in the afternoon. Look after her, she told me, and gave me two rupees. She was the one who said: The demon king is coming, run away, all of you.'

–Oh, she left her here in the afternoon?

An old woman who came into the town every day to beg, she said, 'It was Moni's mother who ran past us, shouting: Run away everyone, big trouble's coming.'

–Why didn't *she* run away?

–No idea. We came running to the station, everyone said they're coming this way. So we . . . somehow . . .

–Now that you're here, stay. Shut the gate and lock it, Kush. Call me if necessary, I'm awake. Come, Tiger, let's meet our honoured guests.

Sein and Ananda were in the guesthouse on the first floor of the outhouse, the doors and windows tightly shut.

'Open the door,' said Tapan, 'it's Tapan.'

They opened the door. 'Shuku-babu said to keep everything closed,' said Ananda.

–Why, is there some danger?

–So he said.

–What danger? He went home so confidently even in this darkness. Have you eaten?

–Oh yes, all arrangements have been . . .

–Why have you closed the windows? How will you sleep with everything shut?

–It's so loud out there . . .

Tapan took a step forward, looked at them, paused.

–No, it's stopped.

–This kind of thing all of a sudden . . .

–Nothing will happen here. Go to bed.

–We passed that way earlier . . . it was all so peaceful. The sunset was absolutely beautiful . . .

–Narrow escape. That's around when it began. Don't worry, the police are on the spot . . .

–That No. 3 . . .

–Not everyone's a criminal. Never mind, go to bed. You're safe here.

Tapan himself had no inkling then that, soon, there would be no need to keep criminal behaviour concentrated to No. 3. Even demolishing the No. 3s in every small town and big city of India and replacing them with gleaming roads or elegant buildings would not be able to stop criminal activity. It would seep through every pore of society, spread everywhere. Various categories of antisocials would emerge, not all of whom would resort to bombs or marrying Papia, and their multifarious activities would bore into the foundations of society until they collapsed.

The future cannot be seen.

*

The news spread across the town at about seven the next morning. When Goju killed Kalo and went to jail, several thousands of rupees belonging to Kalo had vanished. It was never traced.

–Goju stayed with his trusted associate Habib for two days in Jagaddal. Habib sent some of his own reliable men with Goju. Goju left some money with Habib, it wasn't clear whether it was a payment or a loan or some of Goju's own money. He bought some bombs and a revolver. Then he came to No. 3 with Habib's men.

Kush paused to wipe his brow.

–How did Papia know he was coming?

–Everyone knew.

–And she didn't run away?

–She kept trying to drive Rongeen out. Get out, get out, she kept saying. You think he listened? Then he said: If I have to go, I'll chop you and your daughter before I go. That's when she managed to snatch the girl and take her out somehow. Left her somewhere, then came back and started screaming, warning everyone. Fakir said she seemed to have gone mad. Then she charged at Rongeen with the kitchen blade, slashed his leg even, but nothing helped.

No, it didn't. The assailants scattered and fled, it's true, when the police started firing, but they kept hurling bombs all the while.

–How many died?

–The police are still bringing out the corpses.

–Anyone died by police firing?

–The OC took out a solid fellow. Remember Jagat? Whom Dinu-babu threw out? Who knew all this while he was in Jagaddal with Habib. He's been taken out.

–Let's go downstairs.

*

Downstairs, Tapan told them, 'It's morning, but don't leave just yet.'

Curfew. There was a curfew in No. 3. From evening till dawn. The sub-divisional office, SDO, arrived. And, around ten in the morning, a truck with five bodies. Rongeen, Goju, Jagat, Rongeen's right-hand man Phelan—and Papia. Papia's body was riddled with bullets. A huge crowd gathered outside the police station.

Eleven people grievously injured by bombs and bullets had been admitted to hospital under police watch. Several more were arrested.

The OC rang.

–Is Papia Singh's daughter there with you?

–Why do you need her?

–We need her to identify the body, don't we?

–No, you don't. Everyone in No. 3 knows them. No need to expose a young girl to such a sight. Why must you?

–Those who are there with you might have some information.

–They ran away before sunset. It's the people on the spot who know what happened. But the police had no advance information—you had no idea that such an incident was about to happen.

The OC smiled.

–It's not true that the police had no information. Even when we do, we can't always act. And they came to *you* in the afternoon, but you . . .

–Not in the afternoon but after darkness had fallen. I went to you immediately afterwards.

–Yes, well . . . Jagat . . . Phelan . . . Rongeen . . . Goju . . . that's four criminals taken out.

–Yes. Papia too.

–She was a hard character.

–I know. All right, I'm hanging up now.

'Why are you upset?' said Tiger. 'You're going on about Papia, but if she married Goju first and then Rongeen, she was obviously going to die.'

–She saved her daughter's life, though.

–Cast her adrift, you mean. Who'll look after her now?

–Let the police take care of it. Let them send her to an orphanage.

–What about Papia's house?

–What about it? Why are you fretting?

The monkey-dance man said, 'Where will the girl stay? Everyone knows who she is. If she stays with us, someone is bound to attack her.'

–Attack her?

–Don't forget the house.

Tapan realized that Tiger was right. Only the police could handle this.

The OC said, 'A girl child, after all. Some arrangements will definitely be made for her. What can we do? If the SDO sends a note, we can request an orphanage. She'll end up at Shibtala Orphanage, where I haven't seen any girl coming to any good. How will they? Runs on government grants, the authorities are utterly indifferent. You'd weep if you saw the way they live and dress and eat.'

–Isn't there any place with decent arrangements?

–Not that I know of.

–Let her stay with them for now. If you get some useful information, let me know. They'll bring her to you.

–You really are a very strange man. Who's her mother anyway, and yet here you are, worrying about her.

–Can't be helped.

–Considering her parentage, she'll grow up a criminal too.

–It's true, that's how life is shown in Hindi films. It may happen, it may not. Dinu-babu's brothers aren't like him. His son, not even remotely.

The OC shook his head.

–They're the exceptions. My experience says otherwise. Maybe I can't trust anyone because of my life handling crooks and criminals. Hindi films show a lot of real stuff too.

–Perhaps. Just keep it in mind.

–How can I not, since it's come from you.

A few days later, the OC said, 'There you go, the girl has set you free.'

–What do you mean?

–I was on my rounds there, though that police post at No. 3 is temporary. I don't know what the authorities will decide, but it's going to be impossible without a permanent outpost.

–What happened to the girl?

–She was staying with the monkey-dance man and the old woman. This morning I saw they were all gone. The paan seller said, they left very early this morning. Gone, meaning the entire crowd is gone.

–Gone!

–Yes, sir. A girl child, they're sold off, you know. There's no limit to the kind of things that happen in and around Calcutta. The girl market is thriving.

–Such a young girl.

–Excellent for begging. Or for training by the madams. That business is booming.

As Tiger had said, 'No investment. All profit. Just get hold of them.'

Tapan lapsed into a sullen silence. 'Fate, it's fate,' said Tiger. 'How will you come between a person and their destiny? Don't worry about it, let me take you for a drive.'

–I'm not liking this.

–Rongeen invited his own death.

–I need to talk to Bhabani-babu.

–I heard he's coming.

–It'll be good if he does.

*

Bhabani-babu came with Renu-boudi in his new car. She was going to pray to Shonkota Kali. 'The apple of her eye, her younger son-in-law, has got into the hotel business. Keeps asking for money: 'You can't start a fashionable hotel in Puri with small change. Give me the money, or take your daughter back.'

–Will they give it?

–Why shouldn't they? Every fistful of dirt is being turned into gold.

Renu-boudi came back from the temple dressed in a Benaras-silk sari and gold jewellery. She'd offered hibiscus flowers made of gold and a nose-ring to the deity. She was determined that her heart's wish be fulfilled.

A room in the guesthouse was unlocked. Renu-boudi lay down on the Dunlopillo bed.

–I'm not going to eat, I don't want to do anything.

'Laltu has invited us to dinner,' said Bhabani-babu. 'Will you go?'

–Oh god. There'll be meat everywhere!

–They'll have separate arrangements for you.

–What a bloodsucker his father is. You have tea gardens, so many other things, why can't *you* build a hotel for your son?

–Don't talk rubbish. It's all theirs anyway. Just that you're giving it now instead of later. Do you see me heartbroken?

–So humiliating, those letters of his. Who knows how my baby girl is suffering?

–Where do you see her suffering? The hotel will be in her name. They'll run it together. No, it's a good line, a respectable business. Full of possibilities. If the Bengalis don't get into the hotel business, the Punjabis will take over. Never mind, you should rest. Let me finish my meetings. Do you really see your daughter suffering? She's going on holidays with her husband, can't you see how happy she is?

–You think Debi's father-in-law won't make demands also?

–Give her money too. Whom will you give your money to if not to your daughters? There's no one else. Be quiet now, and lie down for a while.

'A mother's soul, after all,' said Bhabani-babu, emerging from the room. 'Crying her heart out. I just cannot handle women's tears.'

The path from Dinu-babu's residence to the outhouse had been laid with gravel now. With flower plants on either side. The doorman's room was beside the gate within the compound. Rows of plants stood close to the perimeter wall. A small garden fenced off with barbed wire had two kinds of jasmines and balsam roses. No one was allowed to enter this garden which supplied flowers for the puja at Mohanlal-babu's house.

Tapan was in the sitting room behind the office. Dressed in a half-sleeved shirt and trousers, his usual. He looked stronger now, Bhabani-babu felt something had changed. There was a fierceness in his gaze.

–I heard the whole story. Terrible affair.

Tapan looked at him.

–Rongeen was always hot-headed.

Tapan kept looking at him.

–You're not saying anything?

–After you're done.

–I'm . . . saying . . .

–Then let me.

Tapan leant back. Despite Bhabani-babu's presence, he lit a cigarette. 'Nexus,' he said. 'Learnt the word recently.'

–I know what it means, Tapan.

–Once it was between you and Dinu-babu. Now, between you, Sudhin-babu, Laltu-babu, Mohanlal, all the iron-and-cement contractors, even Tiger. All of you together, a different kind of nexus. There's no party behind a nexus, after all, there usually isn't. A party can be used, of course, but the real thing is profit, right?

–Don't be too harsh with me, Tapan. For various reasons, my heart is heavy today.

–It can be, it should. Renu-boudi's younger son-in-law is plotting, it's natural to be upset. But these things need to be said for your benefit and mine. For the benefit of today's nexus.

–Go on, but don't be harsh.

–Why would I, you've given me so much. Anyway. Dinu-babu, Mohanlal-babu and you used to operate behind the

Congress tricolour. It was simple enough for the townspeople to know what was going on. This party has criminals on its rolls too. Who are feared and hated. Sudhin-babu and Laltu-babu were opposed to you then. And you, to them. Dinu-babu used to spout those same old ancient stories, all nonsense. How they weren't part of the movement in 1942, how they bad-mouthed Subhas Bose, how after Independence they had shouted: This Independence is a lie. But yes, back then, the town knew who was in the government and who was not. Identifying a nexus was easy.

–Is there any need to rake up all that?

–There wouldn't have been if you hadn't installed me here. I'll keep doing things on your behalf. But when it's convenient for you, you'll turn me in . . .

–You're a close friend now, Tapan.

–Nonsense! You and I are like a pair of snakes, neither trusts the other. Each of us is looking for an opportunity to show the other who's more venomous. Never mind that. This town. Not everyone here has sold out. They're bewildered by today's nexus. Opponents seem to be opposing each other politically. Mohanlal-babu is a Congress man, you have a label too. But that opposition only goes so far. Where profits are to be made, such a business brings about great unity.

–This is survival strategy, Tapan. A regular affair.

–But the town is confused.

–Done with your speech?

–No, I'm coming to the point. You want to build goodwill now, don't you?

–I do.

–Then you can't keep the hooch business. You can't keep the byarakbaari. You're in business now, stick to business. Why do you need those other things? You have so many projects—why don't you hire all these boys. Tiger's a sharp one. He can manage anything you ask him to.

–Yes, the affair at No. 3 . . . You didn't go.

–You think I'd have been able to stop it if I had? Rongeen was warned repeatedly, he didn't listen to anyone.

–You've built some goodwill for yourself.

–Everyone fears a murderer.

–I'll think about it.

–Think quickly. Oh, and we'll hire locals as labourers. You can see, I'm thinking of nothing but your interests.

–Tiger might be here now, but the byarakbaari goes back a long way. Back to when a British company owned all the mills around it. And where will *they* go if you close it down overnight?

–Tiger deserves better. The woman there can run it. You can keep the ownership if you like.

–I'll think about it. You're a man of principles, I like it. But this line of business will creep into the homes soon. The times are changing. They have to.

–Will things get worse?

–Many more frauds like me will spring up. Cold cash will come into play, corruption will become widespread, you'll see the games being played in India by mega-Bhabanis and mega-Tapans. The times will change.

–Perhaps.

–Here's the truth, Tapan: One person's pleasure is built on five people's misery. Addicts will drink no matter what. Shut this lot down, others will set up another. They'll set themselves up in villages. But yes, I'll tell Tiger that you have his interests at heart.

–Didn't Rongeen have a family?

–He did, but they disowned him long ago. Stubborn as a mule, all his life. How strange! No one in this line is interested in what happens to anyone else . . . Don't trust Tiger so much.

–I'm telling you again, he deserves justice. He's close to his family.

–Would he have joined us if that were really the case?

–And you people need to take a permanent decision on No. 3, tell the SDO, tell the police too.

–I'll tell them. Have you considered politics?

–What about it?

–To survive, you have to align yourself to one of the parties.

–I won't go to any of them, forgive me.

*

'Spoken like a man,' said Tiger. 'The fact is your popularity is growing, they're worried about it.

–I spoke about you, you should know.

–Many thanks, Dada. I'll get a little respect if it happens. You've seen what it's like, Dinu-babu and Irani died, then Rongeen and Goju the other day, so many people, everyone said: Good riddance to evil. Running dirty businesses and shooting people earns no one any respect.

–They'll have the bands out on the streets if I die.

–Why should you die? What about the vegetable sellers and hawkers and shopkeepers who say: We're doing business in peace now, thanks to Tapan-babu?

–The Dalits will never say the same.

–Not true. Many people are pleased at the hooch dens being shut down. Of course, they will always be unhappy about Bharat.

–Yes . . . they will.

Tapan lapsed into silence.

–Don't you go home at all?

–Haven't been in a long time. Why're you suddenly asking?

–You're in a different mood when you've been home. You start brooding otherwise.

–Have Bhabani-babu and Renu-boudi left?

–They're leaving tomorrow morning. There's a meeting tonight at Laltu-babu's. Said they'd discuss No. 3, cleaning up the town. From what I can tell, they'll get rid of the small operators.

–Let's see. Papia and her girl couldn't be saved. That's sad.

–Who can save anyone, Dada? Are you god?

*

–God, you're god.

The woman was sobbing, slapping her forehead. About twenty-two. Small eyes, full lips, back-combed hair, tightly knotted. A printed sari, rubber sandals, clutching a nylon bag.

–You're god, save me.

Shobuj was standing at a distance, looking away. 'Stop crying,' Tapan said sternly. 'Speak clearly. Who's this, Shobuj? What's your name?'

–Radha . . . Karmakar . . .

–Where are you from?

She began to weep again.

'Tenibag, beyond Kusumpur,' said Shobuj.

Tenibag! Where they once made superior hand fans and decorative palm-leaf mats. Fans in various designs, so beautiful they were included in bridal trousseaus. The palm-leaf mats were multicoloured, and even been awarded at an art exhibition. Tapan and his friends would go to Tenibag for the fresh palm juice. There were several Karmakar families—they were black-smiths, crucial to rural life. The blacksmiths of Tenibag were quite well-to-do. Tenibag was also advanced when it came to education, with a number of college and high-school graduates among its residents. Apurba Karmakar even used to work at a bank.

–If you're from Tenibag, what are you doing here?

'Go, sit over there,' said Shobuj, 'Let me explain.'

The woman sat down at the foot of the stairs. Kept wiping her tears and looking at Tapan, as though he was the master of her fate.

'She's a good girl,' said Shobuj softly. 'Father's dead, brother doesn't work much, it's a poor family.'

–That's not why she's here, Shobuj, tell the truth.

–There was a boy she'd fallen in love with.

–She's old enough, but not married yet?

'I was,' said the woman through her tears. 'He's thrown me out.'

–Where's he from?

–Nabal.

–When did you get married?

–Seven years ago.

–How long were you there?

–He sent me home for the eighth-day ritual, never took me back.

–What's his name?

–Arun Sarkar. Runs shallow-well pumps.

–Why did he send you back?

–My brother couldn't give him a cycle . . . gold buttons . . .

–Did you try to go back?

–We got married so long ago, babu, he won't take me back any more.

–Why are you here? Who's the other boy? Name and address?

–He was doing electrical work in the village for several months . . .

–And so you fell for him?

–He said he'd marry me . . .

Her voice grew very faint.

–And of course you believed him?

–He'd keep coming, told my brother too . . .

–Your brother didn't get you married to him?

—He washed his hands off the whole thing. He said: If we organize a wedding in the village, we'll have to invite everyone, they'll all talk. So Swapan said . . .

—His name is Swapan?

—Swapan Biswas, he'd said. Lives in this town, is an electrician. He gave me an address. Borrowed two hundred from me last Sunday . . .

—How did you get two hundred rupees?

—It's my money . . . I work for myself . . . boiling paddy . . . I have some ducks and hens too . . .

—He asked you to come here?

—Yes, gave me an address. Told me to wait at the Shonkota temple, we'd get married. He lives alone, there wouldn't be any problem.

—And now you've found he was fooling you?

She burst into tears again.

—Why have you come to me?

—He said he'd wait at the temple . . .

—When?

—In the morning. I've been all over, looking for him. All lies, every word. False name, false profession, false address. Finally, some people said: What's the use of going to the police? They mentioned your name, they said you can do something.

—What can I do?

–This is his photo, babu, people are saying he lives somewhere in this town, his name is Aalok Mandal.

Tapan took a look at the photograph. 'Leave this with me, I'll make enquiries,' he said. 'Can't you go back home?'

–My brother will kill me.

–Don't you have anywhere to go?

–I'll jump in front of a train, where else can I go?

Tapan beckoned to Shobuj. 'Where can we let her stay for the night? Your place?'

–Ma won't let her in.

–Take her to my place. Tell Ma to let her stay tonight.

–And then?

–Malay hasn't been in the town for some time, isn't that right?

–He's in Calcutta.

–Take a look at the photograph? Isn't it Malay without the moustache?

–Of course not, where's the scar on the forehead?

–That's true. Anyway, take her now. Tell Ma not to ask any questions. You, go with him. You need to file a General Diary with the police tomorrow.

–The police?

–A complaint must be registered. Your complaint. Now, go with him.

–Please don't send me back to my brother. You don't know him, he'll kill me.

–Go with Shobuj. Don't say anything, keep mum. Shobuj, tell Ma I'll go home today. After I've been to the police station.

*

'Let me see the photograph,' said the OC. 'Why're these cases cropping up so often these days?'

'Can't identify him,' he said after a look. 'But the electricity board should know.'

–He doesn't work there.

–The work's done by contractors now. They take on people as needed, work through labour contractors. Never mind. What's the case here?

Tapan explained.

–You should have brought her to the police station. Who takes such people home?

–Where will a woman stay here?

–In the lock-up, obviously.

–You know quite well what happens there.

–That's true. Very true. But not always.

–Look, there have been rapes in the lock-up here.

–Yes, the local papers ran some reports. Tirtha-babu and the rest of them protested. Nandita Datta demanded a judicial enquiry on behalf of her women's group.

–Yes, her name was Namita.

–And who was she? A confirmed prostitute. Left her home to make money, used to visit the other towns too.

–That doesn't justify rape.

–No, certainly not. The department took steps. The rapist was suspended and transferred. Don't you want to know what happened to the woman?

–What happened to her?

–She was sent to the Liluah rescue home. She ran away from there. And went back to the same business. You simply cannot rehabilitate these women.

–The Liluah home is horrific!

–Let the government take care of all that. Send the woman, she must lodge a complaint. And look at the state of the police station, look at the arrangements for women here. And you know what, there's poverty everywhere, all kinds of temptations. There's easy money in this business, many women are joining it.

–Yes, they are.

–And why not? Even village people have become greedy. I know of cases where wives make money from this line of work. The husbands know full well, accept it.

–This woman's saying she's been cheated with a promise of marriage.

–This is commonplace. The men come from Bihar to get married. They pay the girl's guardians some money, spend some more on a wedding. Then they sell the girl off to a brothel.

–Where?

–Calcutta, Patna, Bombay, Delhi, absolutely everywhere. Trafficking in women will keep growing, you'll see. From Bombay, they even send them to the Gulf countries.

Tapan felt a searing pain in his head. As though he had an invisible haemorrhage. Was society in the grip of a terrible cancer?

'So much of it happening along the border,' the OC continued. 'And why shouldn't it? No investment. Cash if you sell them, cash if you get them into brothels. This is a business with no losses.'

It was true, Tiger had said as much the other day.

–Touts everywhere. How do women turn up at the byarak-baari otherwise? And once they're in, they know there's no point getting out. It's not so hard, after all, to break free. But even if they do, their families won't take them back. They have to return to the same business. There are exceptions, of course. A fruit trader in Calcutta is happily married to a former whore. I know it for a fact.

–Very well, I'll send her.

–Don't come yourself, just send her. You have a good reputation.

–This proves a cancer has overtaken society. An infamous murderer has a good reputation! Do you know Shibtosh Dutta?

–No, before my time.

–He built three primary schools in the town. Picked children off the streets and educated them. That Ranjan's garage? Shibtosh-babu was the one who made him a motor mechanic. But he fell ill with some unknown disease, vomiting, rashes, high fever. He suffered and suffered, died more or less without treatment. He was the one who should have the good reputation. But no one even knows his name. And look who's famous instead! Me! This town is rotten to the core. I'm going now.

*

The house had been freshly painted, the cracks on the wall that looked like the map of India were gone. There were grilles on the doors and windows, a new kerosene stove in the kitchen. Tapan's mother had arranged some things in the cupboard built into the wall. The books he had won as prizes for elocution. Small, discoloured trophies he'd won at sports. A set of small glasses Suku and Buku had won at a three-legged race. Books from their school days. Tapan's essay-competition prize, *The Mountain of the Moon*. Reba's textbooks, music notebook.

Tapan's eyes stopped at one of the photographs.

His mother had a photograph taken at Banbihari Studio with her four children. Reba clutching the end of her sari, Suku and Buku on either side, Tapan behind her. She was dressed in a white sari with a broad green border. The boys wore freshly washed shirts and shorts.

–Why have you kept these, Ma?

–I look at them, touch them. Feel all of you close to me.

–Did the girl come?

–Yes, I'll let her sleep in my room. Who's she, why did she come to you?

–Everyone keeps sending whoever they can to me. Am I god, can I solve everyone's problems?

–You must have been able to help some people, that's why they send more. So many of them ask me too.

–Don't promise anyone anything.

–I don't.

–You look different in your new glasses.

–I can see much better too.

–How could you have neglected something like your eyes?

–Shobuj also said I look different.

–He's a really good boy.

–Shyamal's mother says Shobuj has gone to hell. Shobuj tells her so many people say such good things about you. She keeps quiet then. Shobuj tells her: Don't you see, women aren't scared to move about the town any more? She doesn't reply. The fact is, she can't forget that Shyamal had to go away. They're well, Shobuj tells her, they'll take you to live with them as soon as they've settled down.

–Does Shobuj give his mother any money?

–He gives a bit, saves a bit too. That's good. You should save too, it'll prove useful.

–That reminds me. Listen, I'm taking you to Calcutta tomorrow.

–So suddenly?

–I'll put the money in a joint account with you. I don't need to know what you do with it. Your sons can buy land, build houses. My only condition is that the houses should belong to you.

–What about this house?

–I'll sell it, Ma.

–Your father owns it.

–Let him take the money. He was so greedy for money, but never saw any.

–And then?

–Baba and you mustn't stay here. I'll be at peace if I know you're somewhere else. The town is a different place now, Ma. This matter of No. 3 won't be solved easily. If you move to Ranaghat, no one will attack you for being my mother.

–How much money, Tapan?

–A lot, Ma. There's so much money in this land business. Reba and Shyamal can look for land too, if they want. And you can always build a small house near Calcutta yourself.

–So much money!

–Yes, Ma. And if you don't want that, let Suku and Buku build houses where they are. I'm telling you again, all this is money from the business.

–The houses can come later.

–No. My life has no guarantee.

–Do you know banks in Calcutta?

–The bank here will give me an introduction. I'll open an account, then transfer the entire amount.

–Whatever you think is right.

–It's safest for you not to live here.

–Does that mean I'll never see you again?

–I can visit you, you can visit me too. But I don't want to visit, it's best for me not to cast a shadow on their lives. Let everyone live happily where they are. Everyone knows they have no relationship with me—let it stay that way.

–If only you'd got married.

–Think of Dinu-babu's wife and children.

–Won't ask you again.

–Aren't you asking me to eat tonight?

–Oh . . . all this talking . . .

Tapan's mother laid a place for him on the floor, brought out the food.

–What about yours?

–I'll eat with Radha. She knows how to run a home. She swept the floors, sliced the vegetables. Quite a sweet girl.

–Is she quiet now?

–She's crying a lot: What will happen to me.

–How can I tell.

–The girls have to bear all the pain. They're set adrift, their lives are ruined, happens all the time.

–The brother's inhuman. Didn't even try to find out anything about the boy.

–Very true.

–What's this? You've made payesh?

Tapan's mother smiled wanly. 'It's your birthday. I've never managed to . . .'

–Shobuj likes sweets.

–I gave him some. Tapan?

–What?

–Can't you marry this girl?

–No, Ma. I'll never have a normal life. I don't even think about such things.

–And tomorrow?

–Shobuj will take her to the police station to make a complaint.

–No, I mean, are we going to Calcutta tomorrow?

–I'd like to. I've checked with the bank, they'll write a letter, that's all we need. We'll go in the car, Ma.

–To Calcutta, that too in a car!

–Why not!

–The girl?

–She'll stay here. She can come back here from the police station. Radha!

Radha appeared. She had changed into a different sari, plaited her hair. An imitation-gold nose ring. He face and eyes were still puffed up from all the crying.

–Don't send me to the police.

–You have to go. Tell them everything—why you're here, how you came, what brought you to me. I can't have you stay here permanently. Nor can I send you away unless proper arrangements are made. Do as I say.

–Ma needs help, I could stay here.

–I can't do that, there are other constraints.

Radha went away slowly. 'She's studied as far as Class Six. She could get a job like mine at the hospital. She could help Sumana and the others, stay there.'

–She can if she wants to. See if you can help. But she can't stay here.

–She'll do whatever you ask her to.

–She hardly knows me.

–She trusts you.

–That's a mistake, Ma. Once she gets a job, she mustn't come here at all. I told you didn't I . . . who knows when someone will do something. I'd better go now.

–You've come after a long time.

–Yes.

Tapan was trying to stop these visits entirely. He had to. The Tapans of the world never put down roots once they went into this line of work.

The Tapans were instruments in others' hands. Knife-wielding instruments. The men who owned the Tapans, they were safe. They had everything. Renu-boudi, Renu-boudi's daughters, gleaming houses, sacred food fit for the gods, masseurs in the morning, controlled diets, meetings and conferences, starched and spotless clothes.

The Tapans were covered in blood. This too is a cancer, Ma. They need the Tapans, the Tapans need them. When their numbers will grow, they will manufacture countless Tigers and Rongeens. That's when the Tapans will become redundant. Or perhaps the Tapans will remain important even then. The future is unknown, Ma.

–I'll go now.

*

The people at the local bank wrote an introduction for their Shyambazar branch in Calcutta.

–You want to withdraw the entire amount?

–No, I'll leave about ten thousand.

–A loss for us.

–It will go up again.

–Wait, let me make this one a joint account too. It'll be easier for your mother.

Tapan felt a weight slide off his chest. No matter what happened to him, his mother wouldn't suffer financially.

–Are we going in the jeep?

–It's the best car, Ma.

They reached Calcutta around noon. Because of traffic, they got to the bank only around one. The account was opened. Putting in five hundred in cash to start it off, Tapan then deposited his cheque, for five lakhs, eighty thousand, six hundred and seventy-seven rupees. And felt so relieved.

–You'll never have to worry again, Ma.

–No, and nor will you.

–It's quite late, let's go eat something.

–You'll eat too, won't you?

–Some sweets . . .

–That's best.

After they had eaten, Tapan said, 'Let me take you somewhere.'

–Reba's house?

–I don't even know where it is, and I can't go there either. Neither Shyamal nor Reba will be pleased.

–They haven't really understood you.

–Perhaps they're the only ones who have.

Tapan's mother was entranced by Dakshineshwar. She looked as happy as a little girl.

–Just like I saw in *Rani Rashmoni*, Tapan.

–Of course, Ma. Come, let's walk around, look at everything. We have to go back in a bit. So many beggars here, what a crowd. Do you want to give them some money? Here, take some.

They walked around, looked at the different parts of the temple.

–Even the Ganga is so beautiful here. How peaceful it all is.

–You've never seen this before?

–How would I have? Did anyone ever bring me here? I've been stuck there all my life. I didn't go anywhere when you weren't there, just spent all my time at the Shonkota Kali temple. I'll always remember this day.

She bought a large box of sandesh, offered it to the deity and had it blessed.

–I'll take the sweets home for everyone. Shobuj and Biru and the rest of them come now and then. The girl too. Your father . . .

Tapan's mother sighed. Helplessly, she said, 'He's a changed man now.'

–Good.

–This house to be built, he'll live there too, won't he?

–Everything will be as you want it. You can hardly leave him alone anyway. For now, it's going to be deposits and withdrawals from the bank in the town. The money here may grow. But, as I said, the house will be yours, they'll inherit it afterwards. They won't disagree, why should they?

–And the rest of this money?

–The interest is your income. You can distribute it among them later as you see fit. Everything belongs to you now, they will take care of you. And, Ma!

–Yes?

–Give some of the money from the town account to Kush and the others. Those four boys really take care of me.

–I will, Tapan. Now that you have some money, can't you just go away?

–No, Ma. Bhabani-babu will go to the police if I try. And then . . . Let's go, don't worry about it.

–Don't worry. So easy to say.

–What's the use? Do you and I control anything?

*

Shuku-babu and the others had observed the whole incident. 'That girl came,' Bhabani-babu said, 'and now Tapan is putting his money away. Do you suspect anything?'

–He's got nothing going on with the girl.

–Why's he moving his money?

–It's for his mother.

–Some other plan? Is he planning to run?

–How would I know? You know what they say about the mind and its secrets. But Dada knows he can't get away, he's told me so many times.

–What if he takes protection from the police?

–I doubt it. He's not one to run away. He broods, keeps to himself. Doesn't drink, doesn't entertain women. He's a strange type. He could have had Sumana if he'd only said the word.

–These are the dangerous ones, you know. Imagine not drinking or having fun at his age. He does none of it?

–No.

–What do the people say?

–To the poor he's god. He tried to save Papia's life, he protected Sumana's honour, he's helping this woman too. These things get about, after all. Abhik and Somjit are wary of him. Everyone knows you can go to him for justice. He stopped the molestation at the hospital, after all.

–You seem to be a fan too.

–He said: This is a time for big business. People will be happy if we stop the small shit, then they won't remember the bad things we do. We have to be gentlemen now.

–He said so?!

–So many people have booked flats because he said so. The locals will be happy also, if they're taken on as labour.

–We'll see. But not everyone is happy with honest money. Big money comes in faster through other means. It goes away too, but who keeps that in mind? People forget things easily.

–That's true.

–We have to keep an eye on him, that's the main thing. I didn't know he was so attached to his mother.

'Mother and son,' said Tiger. 'It's natural.'

–Who will look after the byarakbaari if you move here?

–I'll make arrangements. We can lease it out to Mashi.

–What's this girl like?

–Haven't seen her.

–Who knows, maybe Tapan's fallen for her.

–He'll never walk that path.

–What's her name?

–Radha.

*

Radha was tired of waiting at the police station. The OC simply wouldn't make time for her. By the time it was her turn, she was stiff with fear and anxiety.

The OC had a deep voice.

–Your name is Radha Karmakar?

–Radharani Karmakar.

–Then why did you say Radha?

–That's what everyone calls me.

–You're from Tenibag?

–Yes, babu.

–Who else lives there?

–My brother.

–What's his name?

–Pabanchandra Karmakar.

–You were married?

–I was.

–Why didn't you stay with your husband?

–He sent me back in a week.

–You didn't go back?

–He married someone else soon after.

–Why did he send you back?

–My brother couldn't get him a cycle.

–How did you meet this man?

Radha told him all about it, about everything that followed.

–You were wrong to leave your home for him.

–Said he'd marry me.

–So you came away? Go on, write it all down. What if we catch him?

–I'll marry him if he agrees.

–Unnecessary trouble. What made you turn to Tapan-babu?

–Everyone said: If anyone can help, it's him.

–Yes, do as he says. If we get some information, we'll let you know. You look like you're from a decent family. Why did you have to jump onto the first man you saw? Don't you know what they do with women with false promises of marriage?

–No, I don't.

Tears trickled down Radha's cheeks.

–We'll make enquiries in Tenibag too.

–Don't tell my brother, please.

–What if he wants you back home?

–He won't.

Radha shook her head. 'Wasted away his blacksmith's business. His wife and I worked on the fields, on the farms, in the other people's houses, but he didn't care. I made a living for myself, still he kept telling me: Get out, get out.'

–Anyway, inform the police if you go anywhere. Not planning to run off somewhere, are you?

–Where will I go? Ma said she'll get me a job as an ayah at the hospital. I'll work there.

–Ma?

–Babu's mother.

–You're calling her Ma too? Very nice. Yes, best to work for a living. All right, you may go now.

*

–That was Tapan-babu's candidate, understood?

–He helps everyone.

–True. I wouldn't have got a flat in the housing colony without his help. Small, yes, but something of my own.

–I'll ask for one too.

–Despite that huge house of your father-in-law's?

–Who wants to live so far away in Cooch Behar? This is near Calcutta, convenient for the girls' schools too.

–See if it works out.

*

Tapan's mother did her best to get Radha a job. The matron proved to be a pleasant surprise.

–Of course, Hashi-di, since you're the one asking. Let me note down her name. Will she agree to do night duty?

–In the female ward, please.

–Where will she live?

–Let me ask Sumana.

Sumana and her colleagues agreed at once.

'Do your work here properly,' said Tapan's mother, 'you'll get work at the nursing homes too.'

Radha bent low and touched her forehead to the old woman's feet. Tapan's life won't be a normal one, his mother thought yet again, but it could have been.

–Don't spend time with any and every one, don't even talk to them. The town isn't a good place.

–Yes, Ma, I won't forget.

–Many men will try to tempt you with promises of marriage. Don't get fooled, they're all cheats.

–Yes, Ma.

But Radha wasn't able to keep her word. In their bid to please Tapan, the police kept its enquiry going and caught Deba Pal, aka Swapan Biswas. The police took Radha to see him, and she was horrified. They had beaten him up so badly, he was barely recognizable.

'All I did was change my name,' Deba said. 'Otherwise, Radha . . . the accident I had that day . . .'

–What happened?

–A bus accident near Mirpalashi, Radha.

–Where did you get hurt?

–Hips, head, hurt a lot.

'An accident near Mirpalashi?' said the OC. 'When? And why did you change your name?'

Deba was silent.

–Look, Radha. This man is a cheat through and through. You can file a case against him if you like.

–I can't.

–Tapan-babu might however . . .

–Why bother him?

–It's my responsibility to inform him. Anyway, do you recognize this man? Tell us.

–Yes, I do . . . Why did you say you'd marry me? So many lies for so long . . . Even your name is false?

Deba doesn't answer.

–I've lost my home. You tell Tapan-babu, please, babu. I'll do whatever he says.

*

Tapan was astonished. 'What are you saying? You're ready to marry him if he agrees?'

–If he's honest from now on . . .

–Are you speaking from your heart?

*

–Radha! Say yes, Radha. I'll do as you say. Give me a chance, sir. I went bad because of bad advice. I'll be good from now on.

–I don't believe you.

Radha lifted her pleading eyes.

–Used a false name, made off with your money, lied to you. There's been no accident in Mirpalashi recently. The last one was eight months ago. Even after all this, if you . . .

–If he stays here, he'll mind his ways out of fear of the police.

–How will I keep an eye on him?

'Everyone knows you, sir,' said Deba.

–How will you support her?

–Electrical work. I have all the tools.

–Where are you from?

–Chakda. I don't go there any more.

–Anyone knows you in this town?

–Samanta-babu, the contractor. Knows me as Deba.

–Whatever you decide, Radha.

–Who else will marry me?

–You have a job.

–I won't quit. I'll keep working even after marriage.

–See what you want to do. Since you're so keen. Where will you live?

Deba Pal fished out some money and a silver chain.

–This is her money. I came looking for her because I want to marry her. Came to the police too, just for her. How would I know she'd filed a complaint against me?

–You didn't go to the police—we caught you.

–Yes, sir.

'Can't you tell the truth, ever?' said Radha.

–One false step and you'll be dead.

Deba trembled.

–I won't, I touch your feet and swear.

–Where will you live?

–In the slum behind the hospital.

–Over there?

–Or in the Dalit slum. I'll get a shanty somehow.

–Radha. Think it over.

–What do I think over, babu? This is my fate. If destiny wills it, he will change and make a home with me.

–Think about it.

And so Radha Karmakar and Deba Pal were married. Everyone in town said no one but Tapan could have pulled it off. Women in these situations usually drifted away. But this one had a future now.

But Tapan wasn't entirely sure of Radha's redemption. Would marrying a man like this lead to anything good?

Still, they got married. Sumana and the other nurses gave them gifts of a cooking stove and kitchen utensils. Tapan's mother gave Radha new clothes, new shoes. 'Nothing more is unnecessary,' Tapan told her. 'People begin with far less.'

Radha and Deba began their married life in the slum behind the hospital. Deba was spotted in Samanta-babu's office. He told Deba, 'Tapan is the boss hereabouts now. Don't try any tricks. If he uses his knife, the police won't even raise their eyes to notice.'

–I won't, sir.

–How many wives before this one?

–Radha doesn't know, sir. Please don't . . . none of them stayed, each of them ran away. That's why I found a village girl . . .

–Ran away or sold by you?

–No, sir, I swear by Kali . . .

–To hell with you. I better not get into trouble because of you.

–No, sir.

–Enough playing around. Time now for . . .

–Yes, sir.

SIX

In the meantime, Malay turned up in the town. 'I was working for Bhabani-da in Kharagpur all this while,' he told Tapan.

Malay had become harder, stronger. His gaze, his tone, both were now very rough. Somewhere inside him, he seemed to have acquired a sense of self-confidence.

–You may have heard, I'm to be a part of the new project.

–I've heard.

–You're supervising the housing project. See if you can fit yourself here too.

–Just one condition: no theft. You have to ensure that.

–Oh, that's a guarantee.

–It has to be done very well, Malay. So that the company becomes a success.

–Of course. Is Tiger still . . . ?

–Yes, but he'll come away.

–I hear you're a god to the townspeople.

–Nothing like that. Where will you stay?

–Let's see. Have you given up knifing?

–You could say so.

–I'm back after a long time, let me take a walk around the town.

–Harassing women has stopped too.

–Are we turning into saints?

–No, we're building goodwill.

–As you say. You're the boss, after all.

*

Bhabani-babu had brought in Malay. Which meant he was unable to control Tapan. Which meant what he needed was an obedient boss. Someone who wouldn't speak harshly to him, nor see through his plans.

'Be very careful, all of you,' Tapan told Shobuj. 'This one's much more dangerous than Tiger.'

–What can he do to you?

–He won't confront me directly.

–Don't worry.

–I'm not worried.

But two days later, the morning news did have Tapan worried.

*

Shobuj rushed to the site on his cycle.

−Radha hasn't been to work this morning. She's not at the hospital, nor in the nurses' quarters.

−Maybe she's at home.

−Neither of them is at home. The door's open, all their things are still inside.

−What's going on?

−Gone.

−If both of them are gone, then there's nothing to worry about. What's Samanta saying?

*

'He's not been coming to work,' Samanta said. 'He's not one to stick to a job. He's been married twice earlier, apparently both the wives left him. My feeling is Deba's up to something.'

−Why didn't you tell me all this earlier?

−He came to me only after he had married her. He works for me, I'm concerned with his work. What do I care what he's doing at home? Why are you worried anyway? You thought it best to get them married, end of story.

−I didn't get them married—she wanted to marry him.

−Then that's that. She's an adult, not a child. Why are you worried?

That's what Tapan's mother said too. 'Why are you worried?'

–Was she happy being married?

–Very happy. She used to worship her husband, as though he had done her the greatest favour by marrying her. She was at the Shonkota Kali temple just the other day, making offerings to the goddess. He goes to the market every day, she said, looks after her.

–Where could they have gone?

–How would I know?

'This is my fate,' Radha had said with so much faith.

–How could she have married him?

–She was desperate to get married. Once a girl walks out of her home, which man will marry her? It's always hard for women, Tapan.

–Nothing has happened to make them leave.

–What's the use of worrying?

For the next few days, this was all that was talked about in the town. It was even rumoured that Tapan had wanted to marry Radha.

'Let's see if the body turns up somewhere,' said the OC. 'I'm told he's done this kind of thing before.'

–It's the wife that leaves him every time?

–So he claims. How will we know? Wives do run away from their husbands nowadays.

–Is this a recent phenomenon?

–Yes, suddenly society is breaking apart, forming new shapes. Such a permissive society among the upper classes, how do you expect the lower classes not to be influenced? Even the women have realized their market value.

–Haven't you seen anything good in your time?

–I have indeed. The husband was about to sell his step-daughter, the wife murdered him to save the girl.

–What punishment did she get?

–She was jailed. Took the girl along with her.

–How strange!

–The end of the story isn't all that good. She got out when she was about twenty-eight. Then she sold the girl and ran away with someone.

–Radha wasn't like that.

–There were problems. He used to bring in other women, Radha used to shout at him.

–Why didn't she tell me?

–She feared for her husband's life.

–Yes. She couldn't trust me either, I think.

–She was afraid of you.

–Who incited Deba to be so bold?

–You should forget about them. It could also be that because you got her married, someone with a grudge against you . . . This could be a trap, Tapan-babu.

–You aren't telling me the whole story.

–Things are calm now, let them stay that way.

–I'll find out the truth, no matter what. Radha's matter isn't personal, but she had depended on me. And I'm not going to tolerate the exploitation of women.

*

To Tapan's surprise, it was Sumana who brought the news.

–You?

Sumana held out a piece of paper. 'I can't tell you anything. Not even how I found out about this.'

–What's this! Deba's sold off Radha! She's in the byarakbaari now!

–Yes, Malay-babu gave Deba three thousand rupees. Deba's done it before.

–Why didn't Radha run away?

–He told her they'd be moving into a new house, that's how he took her there. But I think he made her unconscious first.

–Deba did this!

–He didn't forget the police complaint, nor the beating he got. It's a long story.

–How do you know all this?

–Everyone in the slum knows. They daren't speak up because they're scared of Malay-babu. Apparently, he's come into the town to get rid of you.

–He's come all right, but he won't get out. How long has it been?

–Ten days at least. But I only found out everything yesterday.

Radha was in the byarakbaari! How had Malay grown so bold?

Bhabani-babu, Bhabani-babu.

No one had spoken as many harsh words to him as had Tapan.

Was Bhabani-babu frightened of him, then?

Had Tapan grown too powerful too soon? But Tapan cannot live by swallowing such an insult, he'd rather die. And he'll kill first, then die.

Who else knew in the town? How many of them had kept it from him?

The byarakbaari. Tiger. Mashi in charge. A woman in each room.

Tapan became the tiger now.

–Kush! Shobuj! Kshiti! Biru! I'm going to take action.

–Where?

–The byarakbaari.

–What should we do?

–If you want to live, then run. If you come with me, you might die. You're young men, all of you. Leave the town. Get out. Go somewhere else, try and lead a normal life.

'I'll go with you,' said Shobuj.

–To die?

–You're the one who gave me life. At least I lived a little. Lived my dreams.

Lifting his face to the sky, Shobuj burst into laughter. Tapan had never seen him laugh like this.

–Shobuj!

–Yes, Dada?

–Have they painted the Shonkota Kali temple?

–Not that I know of.

Tapan looked out of the window. At the late-afternoon town. People on the streets, a group of boys running about with a football. Office-goers cycling back home from Calcutta. A snatch of a song drifted out of Somjit's club house, 'Come, open up, open up this door of darkness.'

How would they open it, how would anyone, any generation? What if opening up one door of darkness only led to another door, to another bigger darkness? Still, some day, someone would break them all down, let in the light. Only Tapan wouldn't be there to see it. If he was, then even when they riddled his body with bullets, even then he would have no regrets.

Because Bhabani-babu would still be alive.

Far from the town, from his secure fortress in Calcutta, he would pick up the phone, make contact.

What changing times? The Bhabani-babus would remain, buy up every speck of dirt, every blade of grass, invent thousands of aliases to hoard their wealth. They were thinking big now, they had powerful people with them. They would swallow the smaller towns first, and then start on Calcutta.

Taking out Bhabani-babu would bring some comfort, but that wasn't the solution.

Let someone come up with a solution. Anyone.

Still gazing into the distance, Tapan said, 'If it hasn't changed already, you must pay a visit to the Shiva temple at the back.'

–It's in ruins.

–You'll see, inside, on the walls, we'd used bits of metal to carve our names. Champak, Sourav, Tapan, Shyamal, Kajal. A long time ago. When we were in Class Seven.

–Why are you telling me all this?

–No one knows. I'm telling you. And . . .

–What?

–Tell Chameli: I didn't want to kill Bharat, but he attacked me. One of us had to die that day. I regret that it was him.

–Why are you saying all this?

–Tell my mother to leave the town.

–I'm not getting a good feeling about any of this.

–Nothing to have a bad feeling about. I'm sorry I couldn't make arrangements for all of you. Take this attache case, give it to my mother. It's for the four of you. Tell her to put it in the bank.

–Isn't this the last payment from Bhabani-babu?

–Let him try and prove it. He can't.

–What are you thinking exactly?

–Nothing. Who knows how the end comes, Shobuj. Get this done. Then we have work to do.

Who could tell which way the end would come, along which thread? Was this why Malay had come? So be it. Radha with her pleading eyes had wanted to marry Deba. But the girl that Tapan rescued, that girl was sold by Deba, that girl was bought by Malay, with Tiger in-between? After all this, who would still listen to Tapan?

–Biru! Kush! Kshiti!

They all came and stood before him.

–You haven't gone?

Biru shook his head.

–Aren't you going?

–We're going with you.

–Wonderful! You want to die?

Silence.

–Go, go away. Malay is coming. He'll eat you lot first. Wherever the police spot you, they'll drop you. Take your money from my mother, get out.

–And go where?

Tapan said in a low roar, his tone rough and unfamiliar: 'You're going to my mother tonight. In an hour. Taking your money. Then leaving this town. Bihar, Odisha, wherever you like. Kshiti has some kind of a brother-in-law in Ranchi, go there. Your life is in your own hands now. Find whatever work you can to earn a living. If you don't go, you're dead.'

–With you here?

–What if I'm not?

It took them some time to understand exactly what he was saying.

Softly, earnestly, Tapan said, 'I've taught you everything. It's all temporary in this line of work. I know what's coming, so I'm warning you all. Go away. Live. It's not a huge sum of money, but you can start something small with it. Go.

–Will we never see you again?

Tapan smiled faintly. 'Too soon to tell, Biru. I've thought a lot about it, before telling you to go. You know I don't waste my words.'

–Should we tell Shuku-babu before we go?

–Tell no one. Get your cycles, go to my house, my mother will give you your money, take it and disappear.

–What about Shobuj?

–He won't go. He refuses to listen. But you listen to me. Whatever else you do, don't join this line.

They left.

Tapan unlocked the safe.

Shobuj returned.

–Did you explain everything properly?

–What have you done! You gave them the attache case, it had twenty thousand in it!

–Mere scraps. I could have given them twenty thousand each. Just don't have the time. Shobuj! Think it over again!

–I have.

*

A motorcycle was best today. The roads of the town receded behind them.

–Tapan-da! Brake!

Somjit, Abhik, Nandita and Bablu were in front of them. Surprised looks in their eyes. 'Sorry,' said Tapan.

The roads slipped and slid away behind them. This is where Champak had fallen. Billions of years ago. Aeons ago. This was the road Reba took to go away to Shyamal. Billions of years ago. This was where Tapan's father would be slumped on a bench, drunk. Tapan would pick him up, take him home. This was the field where Tapan and his friends flew kites made by Bharat's father Dhanu. Green kite versus yellow kite. The town was slipping away behind them. Tapan's mother had walked up and down this road, day after day after day. The town slid away.

Now they entered a serpentine lane. 'Use the bombs,' Tapan told Shobuj, 'but avoid people, avoid shops.'

Every window of the byarakbaari was lit up. Strains of 'Dil na karo zakhm, o bedardi balam' floated out from the paan shop.

The motorcycle stopped.

–Throw a bomb onto the washermen's field, Shobuj.

Explosion, smoke. Terrified people screaming. Shops pulling down their shutters. People running away.

Tapan entered, brandishing a revolver.

–Mashi? Where's Mashi?

One of the women pointed at her room and fled. Tapan kicked open the door.

Mashi and Samanta-babu were inside. Tapan hurled the liquor bottles on the floor, kicked away the glasses. 'Where's Radha?' he asked Mashi.

–Radha . . . Who's she, my dear?

–The one Malay brought here.

–Oh, Rani . . . she . . . she's . . . in No. 7, first floor . . .

–Going to burn this house down today . . .

–Malay-babu is . . . over there.

Tapan kicked open every door, one after the other. 'Run, all of you, get out, the house will burn today. No screaming.' The women raced out, the men too.

–Another one, Shobuj.

A bomb exploded, seemed to rend the sky. People rushed out of other parts of the byarakbaari too. Shobuj felt a strange elation. How was he not frightened?

The door to No. 7 was closed. Radha, loosely wrapped in a yellow saree, trembling. Malay standing before her.

–Malay.

–Watch it, Tapan, I have a revolver.

–Put on your sari, Radha.

–Save me, Tapan-babu.

–Don't you dare, Tapan, I've bought her.

–Really?

Malay lifts his revolver to fire. But Shobuj hurls a stool at him. It dislocates Malay's shoulder. Then Tapan twists that arm, breaks it.

–Firing at me, you traitor!

–You're the traitor! Dinu-babu was . . .

–So devoted to Dinu-babu, aren't you!

Tapan's fierce laughter.

–Go to Dinu-babu, Malay, he's looking for you.

Malay's terrified eyes.

–No, Tapan, no, Tapan.

–If only you'd told me earlier. Did you think you'd take my place? Speak. You used Radha to . . .

–Bhabani . . . babu . . . asked me . . . to . . .

–Not working, Malay, I'm very sorry.

Tapan's knife dances. Malay's throat is slit. A fountain of blood drenches Tapan. He kicks Malay's body.

–Go to Dinu-babu.

Radha was seated on the bed. Eyes wide with terror.

Loud footsteps on the stairs.

'Tiger,' says Shobuj.

–Any bombs left?

–One.

–Take the revolver.

Tapan shuts the door.

–Open the door, Tapan-da.

–You, and who else?

–Your game's over, Tapan-da.

–Who's playing, Malay?

–Doesn't matter who.

–Malay's gone to Dinu-babu. Who will you go to, Tiger? To Irani? Irani wasn't a traitor.

–There's no such thing as betrayal in this game, Tapan-da. I'm helpless. I'm not alone, Tapan-da. Bomba and Thaku are with me.

'Shobuj!' said Tapan. 'If they break open the door, throw that last bomb.'

−Yes, Dada.

−Are you afraid?

−No.

A cry escaped Radha lips. From the other side, they were trying to kick the door down.

−Don't be afraid, Radha. See where Deba's got you!

−You . . . gave me shelter . . .

Tapan sighed.

−I hadn't realized.

−You could have taken me away . . .

−It was you who wanted Deba.

−A family . . . I didn't know then.

−Be quiet. Is that the bathroom door?

−No, it leads to the next room.

−And the door at the back?

−The veranda.

Tapan pushed her out into the veranda. 'Run,' he said in a low voice. And shut the door. The revolver had six bullets. Tapan had bought them a long time ago. He picked up his knife. Signalled to Shobuj with his eyes. Unbarring the door, they stood on either side. Because he had been kicking at it, Tiger fell face first on the floor.

Tapan grabbed him by his hair, hauled him to his feet. 'Behind you, Tiger . . .'

Bomba and Thaku rushed in, firing. Shobuj ran out, also firing. Tiger broke free. A bullet in Tapan's shoulder. Tapan's knife slit open Tiger's belly. Had he been hit in the forehead? Why was there the blood in his eyes? Bullets in his abdomen. 'Run, Shobuj, run,' Tapan said. 'I'm hit, don't stop for me.'

Bomba and Thaku froze for a moment. Tapan threw his knife. Bomba tottered, fell. Shobuj ran back in. A loud explosion in the yard outside. The ceiling collapsed. The smell of gunpowder in the room. Smoke.

Sirens approaching. Shobuj and Thaku fired at each other.

*

Because Tapan was still breathing, they had to take him to the hospital.

'Will he survive?' asked the OC.

−With this injury? Impossible. Shot in the head. Stomach ripped open. Shot in the shoulder. The haemorrhaging alone will kill him.

−Seen the crowd outside? The whole town's here.

Eventually, a thin, dark-skinned elderly woman walked up to them. Her head held high.

−I want to see him.

–Who are you?

–I'm Tapan's mother. He doesn't have long now.

'Six bodies,' the OC said, 'Three felled by Tapan.'

–He could. A murderer, after all.

–Now he can't be brought to trial.

Tapan's mother smiled faintly.

–You're smiling?

–You'd have produced Tapan in court. He's a murderer. But OC-babu, those who made these boys commit murder, they'll go scot-free, won't they?

Silence in the room. A sea of people in the corridor outside. Even Abhik had come, he was standing to one side.

Tapan's mother stood near the door.

–Bhabani-babu put the knife in my son's hand. These people have died, Tapan will die. But more murderers will be brought in by them. A man who kills should of course be held accountable. The murder my son committed today was to save a girl from prostitution. I've always lived in shame in this town. But I have no shame about what happened today, no shame. Those who order these murders, they walk free, OC-babu. What kind of justice is that? Is Tapan alone the murderer? What about Bhabani-babu?

–You'd better go.

–Do you have an answer?

'The Bhabani-babus are murderers too,' said Tapan's mother, her eyes dry, her despair icy cold, 'but no one will catch them.'

The crowd outside began to stir.

'You're leaving?' said Abhik.

–Yes. They'll bring him home, let me go there.

Radha came up to her. Biru, Kush and Kshiti too. Her head held high, Tapan's mother began to walk away. The OC saw the people, saw how the death of a murderer had stunned and enraged them. He saw the murderer's mother walking on, her head held high.

Tapan's mother's words had turned the situation explosive.

Notes to the Translation

PAGE 2 | **Netaji's birthday:** 23 January, birth anniversary of the Indian Independence fighter Subhas Chandra Bose (1897–1945), commonly referred to by the honorific Netaji, who raised and led the Indian National Army against British colonial rule. The day is generally a holiday in his native state of West Bengal, often marked by mock military drills as a tribute to Bose's army credentials.

PAGE 2 | **Mashi:** Aunt, specifically mother's sister.

PAGE 5 | **as long as the Congress was in power:** The Congress party held power in West Bengal from 1972 until 1977, when it lost the state election to a leftist coalition called Left Front led by the Communist Party of India (Marxist). This novel is set in the aftermath of the 1977 election.

PAGE 6 | **Naxal movement:** An extreme-left communist insurgency that has its roots in the 1967 armed peasant uprising at Naxalbari, a village in northern West Bengal. The early 1970s were marked by widespread terrorist attacks mounted by Naxalites across eastern India. In 1972, the Congress party came to power in West Bengal following a controversial state election. The new government resorted to brutal tactics to quell the Naxalite movement, including wholesale use of torture, unlawful detentions and killings, especially perpetrated by the Calcutta Police. In 1977, after the Left Front came to power, most Naxalites, including political prisoners, were granted amnesty and released from jail.

jobs on our quotas: Refers to an affirmative-action policy in India, whereby a certain number of positions or 'seats' in the state-run education system and government employment are reserved for historically marginalized communities.

Joy Bangla: Literally, 'Hail Bengal!', a slogan and war cry used during the 1971 Bangladesh War and subsequently as an expression of pride for and loyalty to Bengal. 'Joy Bangla clothes' likely refers to locally produced garments.

Bouma: Sister-in-law (younger than the speaker), used to refer to a daughter-in-law or, as in this case, a younger brother's wife.

Boudi: Sister-in-law (older than the speaker), used to refer to an elder brother's wife.

Thakurpo: Used to refer to a brother-in-law or husband's brother.

Rani Rashmoni: Rashmoni Das (1793–1861), nicknamed Rani, was a prominent landowner, philanthropist and social reformer in Bengal known for her generosity.

Kaka: Uncle, specifically father's younger brother.

bandit Ratnakar . . . transformed into Valmiki: According to some myths, Valmiki, the legendary writer of the epic Ramayana, began his life as a bandit known as Ratnakar. His transformation into an erudite sage is hailed as a miracle.

Eve teasing: A widely used Indian euphemism for public sexual harrasment of women.

Jagattaran Matth: The sanskrit word *matth* refers to a Hindu monastery or institute.

just let the Congress come back to power: In India, the railways is a department of the central or federal government. In the general election of 1977, the Congress party led by Indira Gandhi was voted out of power at the national level, only to be returned to power three years later in 1980.

PAGE 102 | *Kathamrita*: Refers to *Sri Sri Ramakrishna Kathamrita* (literally, 'The nectar of Sri Ramakrishna's words'), a popular Bengali book by Mahendranath Gupta which recounts, much in the form of a gospel, conversations and activities of the nineteenth-century Indian mystic Ramakrishna, reverentially referred to here as 'Thakur' or lord.

PAGE 114 | **Were you brought up in a mission:** The word *mission* refers to an institute that carries out charitable missionary work. Schools run by such missions, whether Christian or Hindu in denomination, are known to instil habits of simplicity and austerity in their students.

PAGE 125 | **secured a huge quota . . . Got a steel quota:** A reference to government tenders secured by private firms. A hotbed of corruption, the 'quota system' often functioned as the source of funds for the nexus between politics and organized crime.

PAGE 133 | **doms:** A historically marginalized caste in India whose traditional occupation was the disposal and cremation of the dead; part of the Dalit community.

PAGE 155 | **lawaris land:** Literally, 'unclaimed' or 'unowned', the Hindi/Urdu word *lawaris* is used derogatively for drifters, bastards and orphans.

PAGE 159 | **Dida:** Grandma, specifically maternal grandmother.

PAGE 193 | **they weren't part of the movement in 1942:** The Communist Party of India did not participate in the 1942 anti-colonial Quit India Movement organized by the Indian National Congress and led by Mahatma Gandhi. This is sometimes seen as the communists' opposition or apathy towards Indian Independence.

PAGE 199 | **eighth-day ritual:** Known in Bengali as Oshtomongol, the final ceremony of a traditional Bengali wedding in which a couple visits the bride's home on the eighth day after the wedding.